MODI
A GREAT LEADER

SOMASEKHARA PANICKER

NewDelhi • London

BLUEROSE PUBLISHERS
India | U.K.

Copyright © Somasekhara Panicker 2024

All rights reserved by author. No part of this publication may be reproduced, stored in a retrieval system or transmitted in any form or by any means, electronic, mechanical, photocopying, recording or otherwise, without the prior permission of the author. Although every precaution has been taken to verify the accuracy of the information contained herein, the publisher assumes no responsibility for any errors or omissions. No liability is assumed for damages that may result from the use of information contained within.

BlueRose Publishers takes no responsibility for any damages, losses, or liabilities that may arise from the use or misuse of the information, products, or services provided in this publication.

For permissions requests or inquiries regarding this publication, please contact:

BLUEROSE PUBLISHERS
www.BlueRoseONE.com
info@bluerosepublishers.com
+91 8882 898 898
+4407342408967

ISBN: 978-93-5989-374-7

Cover design: Shivam

First Edition: February 2024

About the Author

Shri Somasekhara Panicker, born in Othera, Kerala and educated in Kerala and Delhi, is a former Diplomat. He served in the Ministry of External Affairs for close to 35 years and did postings in our Missions in Dhaka, Geneva, Sana'a, Singapore, Bangkok, Tashkent and Paris. Shri Panicker is a student of Political Science, History, Economics and International Relations and is a keen observer of politics in India. He is widely travelled within the country and has visited more than 30 countries abroad.

Shri Panicker is very passionate to see India leapfrog to become a developed nation and is fascinated with Prime Minister Modi's vision to make India a developed nation by 2047.

Dedicated to the People of India (Bharat)

Acknowledgement

I thank my dear wife, Rajeshwari Panicker, who helped and supported me all along while working on this book.

I also thank my dear children, Udai Panicker, son, and Aishwarya Panicker, daughter, for their loving moral support.

"The great ever perform rarer deeds"
-Thirukkural

Contents

Introduction 1

Chapter I: India at the Crossroads of History 3

Chapter II: Whom to Vote for in 2024 8

Chapter III: Modi a Great Leader 15

Chapter IV: Transformational Schemes 23

Chapter V: Infrastructure Development........................ 30

Chapter VI: India 5th Largest Economy in the World 38

Chapter VII: Health 42

Chapter VIII: Covid 19 – Pandemic 46

Chapter IX: Education... 54

Chapter X: Agriculture and Farmers............................. 60

Chapter XI: Foreign Policy 69

Chapter XII: G-20 Summit... 82

Chapter XIII: India's Digital Revolution 86

Chapter XIV: Making Possible the Impossible 93

Chapter XV: Great Leaders are Great Builders too 99

Chapter XVI: Connecting with People 109

Chapter XVII: Women Empowerment 113

Chapter XVIII: Youth and Sports 120

Introduction

This book is my humble tribute to our Hon'ble Prime Minister, Shri Narendra Damodardas Modi and to our dear country. I have been very closely observing PM Modi for over a decade.Modi's love for the country, his steadfast dedication, determination and single minded pursuit to take the country to greater heights, his total devotion to work and his leadership qualities are all incredibly unparalleled. He is an administrator par excellence. He is a leader with a grand vision for the country and each one of his steps is a building block to make India great.

India is making rapid strides in all areas and Modi has clearly laid down a vision and a roadmap to make India a Developed country (Vikasit Bharat) by 2047, i.e, by the 100th year of our Independence.

India will be going for General Elections this year. BJP and Prime Minister Modi have pitched for a Third term for the ruling party. It is the duty of every Indian to ponder over what is at stake.

Do we continue to march ahead at a scorching pace to become a Developed Nation or we slide back to policy paralysis, corruption, pessimism and leadership tussle? Is it 'Modi hai to Mumkin hai' or 'Idhar Kuch nahi hone ka' (everything is possible under Modi or nothing can happen here)?

Sometimes we get carried away by slogans, freebies, baseless criticism, false promises etc. We should not fall into this trap. We have to go by the proven track record, the results before us. A bird in hand is worth two in the bush.

In the last 9 years and 8 months of PM Modi's rule, we had a Government that was honest, efficient, hardworking, responsible and responsive and singularly focussed on the country's development. We have a Prime Minister who has completely devoted his life for India.

Vice President of India, Shri Jagdeep Dhankar, a legal luminary and an erudite person, described PM Modi as a "Yugapurush". He said "If Mahatma Gandhi was the "Mahapurush" (greatest man) in the previous generation, Narendra Modi is this century's "Yugapurush" (man of this generation) (Hindustan Times, Nov 27 2023). I have no doubt in my mind that Shri Narendra Modi will be remembered as a great son of India after Mahatma Gandhi.

I have tried to present to the reader the transformation India is achieving under the stewardship of Prime Minister Modi.

So, India has a clear choice before it in the 2024 Lok Sabha elections. Shri Narendra Modi.

Somasekhara Panicker

26 January 2024

CHAPTER I

India at the Crossroads of History

India is at the crossroads of History. The last 9 years and 8 months have been unprecedented and transformational for India. From a poverty-stricken, backward, Third world country, India (Bharat) has emerged as a power catching the attention of the whole world. The leading powers of the world want to have strategic relations with New India. Who is the architect of this New India?

The people of India elected Narendra Damodardas Modi, the then Chief Minister of Gujarat as the PM in the 2014 General Elections. After a gap of 25 years, i.e, since 1989, a single party could form a Government on its own. During that period, before 2014, India witnessed Governments with coalitions composed of multiple parties. Parties of contrasting ideologies pulling at different directions resulting in policy paralysis.A feeling of gloom and doom prevailed.

Narendra Modi, India's PM since 2014, was born on 17 September 1950 in a poor family in Vadnagar, a small town in Gujarat. His family belonged to the OBC (Other

Backward Class) community, a marginalised section of Society.

We can clearly say that this young boy grew up facing the harsh conditions of economic backwardness and poverty. To help the family, he assisted his father who was running a tea stall in Vadnagar Railway station. So, Modi in his early life sold tea at the railway station. The hardship in his early days of life taught him the value of hard work and also gave him an opportunity to see the common man's life at close quarters.

At the age of 17, Narendra Modi left home and travelled across India for two years exploring various cultures. This journey also took him to the Himalayas where he had an early encounter with the spiritual aspects of life. He returned home as a changed man with a clear vision of what he wanted to do in life. He went to Ahmedabad and joined the RSS, a Socio-cultural organisation.

He became a Pracharak in RSS in 1972 at the age of 22. Early on in his life he started a tough routine, starting his day at 5 A.M and working till late at night.

During the Emergency in 1975, when the freedoms were curtailed, young Narendra Modi joined the movement to restore Democracy in the country. During the 1980s, Narendra Modi shouldered different responsibilities within the Sangh and emerged as an exceptional Organiser with his organising skills. In 1987, a new chapter began in his life when he was made the General Secretary of the BJP in Gujarat. His efforts brought victory for BJP in the Ahmedabad Municipal

Corporation Elections for the first time. As General Secretary, he also ensured that the BJP was a close second in the Gujarat Assembly Elections in 1990.In the 1995 Assembly elections, Mr Modi's organisational skills ensured that the BJP enhancing it's vote share and the party won 121 seats in the Assembly.

Modi became the National Secretary of the BJP in 1995 looking after Party's activities in Haryana and Himachal Pradesh. As BJP's General Secretary (Organisation), he worked to ensure BJP substantially increasing it's seats in 1998 and it's victory in the 1999 Lok Sabha elections.

In September 2001, Modi received a phone call from the then PM Vajpayee asking him to take over as the CM of Gujarat.

Narendra Modi assumed charge as the Chief Minister of Gujarat on 7 October, 2001. He got a big majority in the ensuing Gujarat State Elections in 2002 and continued to return as Chief Minister in 2007 and 2012 with huge majority.

In 2014, BJP declared Narendra Modi as the PM candidate and in the General Elections, BJP won with a majority. BJP got 282 Lok Sabha seats.

In 2019, with the 5 years of performance and delivery of Modi Sarkar, Modi led the Party to win 303 seats. BJP secured 37.3% of the popular votes.

So, what changed in the last 9 years and 8 months? Everything. Let's start from the basics.Modi brought hope, energy, optimism, nationalistic fervour, vision, enthusiasm and a feeling of "We can do" amongst the people. Governance model changed. From a non-serious, laid back governance to a new, efficient, energetic, responsible, delivery based model with speed and scale began. The administration was galvanised. The entire Government Machinery is working towards a vision, a vision of making India a developed nation by 2047.

A New India is being built. New Infrastructure is being built across all sectors. A call is being given to all Indians to work for a developed, strong, self- reliant and powerful India, taking back our civilizational glory that we lost and forgot over centuries of foreign invasions and rule by foreigners.

India is witnessing a period of renaissance in all fields. Economic, social, political, cultural, scientific, in sports and games and so on.

A national awakening is happening. A new India is in the making. A diverse India is coming together to make a "Great India".

We can see a Mahatma Gandhi "moment" in the Swachh Bharat Mission. A Sardar Patel "moment" with the abolition of Article 370 and integrating J&K with India; a Rajendra Prasad moment in the construction of Ram Mandir in Ayodhya; a Nelson Mandela moment in the abolition of Triple Talaq.

There is also an awakening, a resurgence happening among the Hindus. For a long time in our history, maybe after the time of Shivaji and Ahilyabai Holkar, we have a great leader in the country who is unapologetic about being a Hindu and the Hindu religion is being shepherded. This is a Swami Vivekananda moment.

Such moments but come very rarely in history. That is what we Indians have to realise. The country is going in the right direction. Bharat is taking rapid strides in all spheres. We have a Prime Minister who is working super hard, 24x7, honest to the core, selfless like a yogi, has a vision for the country, delivers on his promises, leads from the front and motivates his Ministers and bureaucrats, his party, BJP and the 140 crore people of India.

In a few months time, we Indians have to decide again, who should lead the country. A proven leader like Modi or can we go for an experiment with some rag-tag coalition of parties whose leader is yet undecided?

I would emphatically say - VOTE FOR MODI.

CHAPTER II

Whom to Vote for in 2024

Our vote is very important. Elections give us a chance to decide on who should rule our country for the next five years. This is the essence of democracy. We know that monarchy and autocracy do not give their people the power to elect their leader. We have seen that in autocratic states, there is only a facade of elections.

It is to the credit of India that we have a robust democracy. After we got our independence in 1947 and became a Republic with the adoption of the Constitution in 1950, we have elected our representatives to the Lok Sabha every five years since 1952, the year when we had our first elections. Barring the Emergency period (1975 to 1977) when the term of Lok Sabha was extended for one year, we had elections to the Lok Sabha every 5 years.

The next General Elections for the Lok Sabha is due in May, 2024. It is time for us to take a decision as to whom to vote for. This is also the time for us to review and decide on the performance of the incumbent government and also to make a comparison with the performance of the present government with that of the previous governments.

In the last nine years and eight months, Indians had the occasion to see the functioning of the Prime Minister, Shri Narendra Modi.

Born in a poor family, Modi rose to become the Prime Minister of India, by dint of his phenomenal hardwork, honesty, uncorrupt and selfless nature, simplicity, nationalistic fervour, connect with the people and popularity, unmatched commitment to the development of India, his discipline, his extraordinary ability to put in amazingly long hours of work, his unparalleled energy levels and many other sterling personal qualities.

I still remember the unbelievable transformation he brought about in the working of the Central Secretariat in 2014 after he became the PM. The functioning of Government Offices that we knew of prior to PM Modi took over, was one of a completely laid back style. Though the official timings were from 0900hrs till 1730 hours, yet the Government staff used to attend offices as they pleased, at their own will. Some came before 9'oclock, some at 9'oclock, some at varying times of the day! There was no punctuality. The joke that used to go around in the Secretariat was that the babu would come at 10'o clock, sign the Attendance Register and leave his coat on the chair as a mark of having come to the office and go for his tea sessions and personal work and the actual output during the whole day would not be much. Professionalism and productivity were not the hallmark of the work culture in the Central Secretariat.

One of the most remarkable steps that PM Modi did after becoming PM was to introduce a biometric based system of attendance in the entire Central Secretariat. In the biometric system of attendance, each Secretariat staff member's time of arrival and departure are recorded and available in the system for the Senior Officers or the Minister to see. A most unprecedented step, completely transformational, was put in place bringing discipline and accountability in Central Government offices. True, many staff members did not like it. But a big step was taken. A change in work culture was brought about.

<u>State of Affairs in 2014</u>

Population -121 crore (2011 Census)

Access to clean drinking water -Less than 33% of the population

Access to toilets -46.9% of 246.6 million households -i.e.115.65 million households

Open defecation -65.21 <u>million</u> households

Percentage of people using public toilets-3.2%

Releasing the 2011 Census Data, the Registrar General and the Census Commissioner, Shri C.Chandramouli had said that "lack of sanitary facilities continues to be a big concern for the country". "Cultural and traditional reasons and lack of education seemed to be the primary reasons for this unhygienic practice. We have to do a lot in this area."

Literacy -74.4 %

Access to telephone- 63.2%

Access to mobile phones- 53.2%

Household Fuel: 2/3 households-i.e., 164.4 million households use firewood, crop residue, cow dung cakes or coal for cooking, putting women to significant health hazards and haprdship. Women are forced to rely on traditional smoking fuels to cook.

Drinking Water: 32% of the households use treated water for drinking. 68% of households use untreated water.

17% still fetch water from a source located more than 500 metres in rural areas and 100 metres in urban areas.

Electricity: 67% of households use electricity

Television: 47.2% of households own television sets

Per Capita Income: Rs 60, 972 in 2011-12.

Food grains production: 250 million tonnes-2011-12

Fiscal Deficit-4.6%

(Census 2011)

Comparing Modi versus Manmohan Singh

	MMS (2004-14)	Modi (2014-2023)
1.GDP	$ 1.8 Trillion	3.7 Trillion
2.World Rank	10	5
3.Per Capita Income	Rs 78, 000	Rs 1, 15, 000
4.Exports	$200 billion	780 billion
5.Metro in Cities	5	20
6.Village Power	40%	95%

7. Express Highways	680 km	4067 km
8. National Highways	25,700 km	53,700 km
9. Railways Length	22,048 km	55,198 km
10. Road Quality	88	42
11. RenewableEnergy	25.7	95.7
12. Unicorns	1	114
13. CostGBData	Rs 200	Rs 15
14. Internet Connection	58.9 million	771.3 million
15. Digital Transactions	4.40%	76.10%
16. IITs	16	23
17. IIMs	13	20
18. Khadi Sales	Rs 2.14 lakh cr	6.69 lakh cr
19. Metro	248 km	860 km
20. Forex Reserves	$303 Billion	600 Billion
21. Railway Electrification	3,874 RKMs	37,011 RKMs
22. MBBBs Seats	51,348	1,00163
23. PG Seats(Med)	31,185	65,335
24. AIIMS	7	22
25. Medical Colleges	387	660
26. Airports	74	148
27. FDI Inflows	$299 Billion	596 Billion

28. Bank Accounts	35%	98%
29. High Speed Rail	0	1 under construction 8 Anticipated.
30. Rail Launch	1.6 year	2 months
31. Sanitation	39%	85%
32. Roads(Rural)	69 km/day	130 km/day
33, Universities	723	1100
34. Mobile Manufacturing	5.8 cr	31 cr
35. Gas Connections	55% of population	90% of population
36. Optical fibre	0.02%	50% of households
37. IT Returns	3.8 Cr	9.37 cr
38. Ease of Business Index	142	70
39. Innovation Indx	76	57
40 E-Gov Index	118	96
41. Tourism Index	65	40
42. Climate Change Index	30	14
43. E-Participation	40	15
44. Defence Exports	1, 000 cr	16, 000 cr
45. OROP	Pending	Done

46. Border Infra	Nil	Developing Fast
47. Rafael fighters	Nil	36
48 Apaches	Nil	22
49. Chinook	Nil	15
50. S-400	Nil	5 sqadrons

CHAPTER III

Modi a Great Leader

How do we describe a great leader?

A leader should

 i. Enjoy the support of his people
 ii. Have an intimate knowledge of the condition, the state of affairs of his people-economic, social, political, cultural and the needs and aspirations of his people
 iii. Have a vision for his people
 iv. Be able to lead the people, persuade them, influence them in all conditions to achieve the vision set for his people
 v. Be able to gear up the Govt. machinery and support of the people to work ceaselessly to achieve the vision set for the people
 vi. Be able to maintain peace and harmony in the country to focus on the development of the country
 vii. Be able to create a conducive atmosphere internally and externally to achieve his vision of development of the country
 viii. The leader should have a connect with the people. He should have his ear to the ground.

In all the parameters above, Modi comes out exceptionally great. In 2014, Modi led BJP to victory winning 282 Lok Sabha seats getting majority on its own without the NDA allies. This was 100 seats more than BJP's historic best earlier in 1999 getting 182 seats.

In 2019, after 5 years of performance, Modi got a sweeping majority of 303 seats in Lok Sabha, winning 37, 3% of popular votes.

These figures show that Modi enjoyed the support of Indians.

Modi's humble beginnings and the economic backwardness of his family taught Narendra Modi early in his life the harsh realities of poverty, deprivation and backwardness. This experience of his life helped him to connect with the poorest of the poor. His travels across the length and breadth of the country, beginning at the age of 17 years and thereon, made a deep understanding in Narendra Modi about the country, its people, their problems, their needs, their social and economic challenges and their aspirations.

Modi has a vision

Anybody listening to his speeches, to people or in parliament or even to foreign audiences, will clearly show that he has a vision for the country. He wants to make India a developed nation by 2047. That is, by the 100th year of its independence.

From speeches to his actions on the ground. Government's plans for each Ministry show that his vision is not limited to speeches but is actually followed up with an action plan for making the country a developed nation.

Right from Day one of assuming charge as Prime Minister, Modi started working hard for the country. His devotion to work is 100 per cent and he expects his team, his Ministers and bureaucrats, also to work with 100 percent devotion. He hardly takes any leave or holiday from his work. He is practically working 24x7.

Swachh Bharat Abhiyan

Narendra Modi started from the most fundamental, the basic requirements of the nation. In his first address from the ramparts of the Red Fort on 15th August, 2014, Modi referred to the unfortunate fact about open defecation in India and how it is affecting the lives of women, especially their health. Modi Government launched the Swach Bharat Mission immediately afterwards on October 2, 2014, the birth anniversary of Mahatma Gandhi, who had famously said" Cleanliness is Godliness". Under Swach Bharat Mission, Modi set the target to turn India Open Defecation Free by 2 October 2019, the one hundred and fiftieth birth anniversary of Mahatma Gandhi.

Swachh Bharat Abhiyan was not only about making India Open Defecation Free but also about making India clean. The Swachh Bharat Abhiyan was turned into a Jan Andolan, a people's movement, by involving people from all walks of life to clean their surroundings, their villages, towns and cities. PM Modi led a cleanliness pledge at India Gate in which about thirty lakh government employees joined. Shri Modi himself picked up the broom and initiated the drive at Mandir Marg Police Station cleaning the dirt. The Prime Minister exhorted people to neither litter nor let others to litter. Such a National Movement for cleanliness was unprecedented in Indian history.

On 2nd October 2019, addressing 20, 000 Swachh Bharat Mission activists at Sabarmati Ashram from around the country, Modi said that Open Defecation had gone down from 600 million in 2014 to negligible. Over 11 crore toilets and 2.23 lakh Community Sanitary Complexes were built across all states and Union Territories under Swachh Bharat Mission(Grameen) and Swach Bharat Mission (Urban) till 16 March 2023 taking the sanitation coverage from 39% in 2014 to 100%. 6 lakh villages declared themselves Open Defecation Free.

Swachh Bharat Mission resulted in 14, 67, 679 Schools having a functional girl's toilet giving an impetus to the enrolment of girls in schools.

PM Jan Dhan Yojana

PM Modi announced the PM Jan Dhan Yojana in his Independence Day address on the 15 August 2014. This was a National Mission for financial inclusion of unbanked people of India to give access to financial services.

When the PM set the target of opening 7.5 crore bank accounts for uncovered households in the country by the next Republic Day on 26 January 2015, there was pessimism and disbelief in the enormity of the task and whether the target would be achieved. However, PM Modi, in his unique working style of setting stiff targets, conveyed to the concerned authorities what he wanted. By March 2015, 14.72 crore Accounts were opened.

51.55 crore Accounts were opened so far and there is Rs.2, 17, 620.21 crore balance in these beneficiary accounts as on 26 Jan 2024. Most of the beneficiary accounts are in the name of women.

8.50 lakh Bank Mitras deliver branchless banking services in the country.

PM Jan Dhan Yojana turned out to be a revolutionary Financial success.

(www.pmjdy.gov.in)

Pradhan Mantri Ujjwala Yojana

PM Modi realised the health hazards faced by women, especially in rural areas who cook in poorly ventilated kitchens using firewood, cow dung and charcoal that emit hazardous gases and chemicals that affected the health of women. He often said that cooking with traditional fuels was as hazardous as smoking 400 cigarettes a day. On 1st May 2016, PM launched the PM Ujjwala Yojana through which LPG connections were given to 10 crore poor households till 31 December 2023. PM Modi visited the 10th crore beneficiary in Ayodhya on 31 December 2023. Another 10 million connections have been announced in the second phase to make universal access to LPG connections.

"Give it Up"

PM Modi called upon the well-to-do Indians to give up the LPG subsidy. About 1 crore people heeded to the

PM's call and gave up the LPG subsidy saving the Government Rs.4, 116 crore every year which helped in the implementation of PM Ujjwala Yojana.

Pradhan Mantri Awas Yojana

Another transformative Plan that Modi Government started was to provide affordable houses to the houseless under two schemes. PMAY-U to the urban poor in the Urban Areas and PMAY-Gramin to the houseless in the rural areas. To achieve the objective of "Housing for All", the Government launched the Scheme on 20 Nov 2016.

Under the PMAY-U, 1.19 crore houses have been sanctioned and 1.13 crore houses have been grounded. 79.02 lakhs houses have been completed. A total investment of Rs.8.11 lakh crore is envisaged under this scheme comprising both Central and state contributions. (pmaymis.gov.in)

Under the PMAY-Gramin, 2.94 crore houses have been sanctioned and 1.63 crore houses have been completed under the scheme. Rs. 1, 47, 218 crores have been released to the states/UTs since the inception of the Scheme.

Jal Jeevan Mission

Modi Government has also launched a visionary plan to provide every household with good quality drinking water supply in adequate quantity on regular and at long-term affordable charges. Under the plan, the Central Government will assist, empower and facilitate States and Union Territories for creation of water supply infrastructure so that every household has a Functional Tap Connection by 2024 and have water in adequate quantity of prescribed quality.

As of September 2024, so far 13 crore rural households have been provided with tap water connections under Jal Jeevan Mission. Thus out of 19.22 crores rural households in the country, 18.93 crores have tap water connection.

Peace and Security

We will look at many other transformational changes in the coming chapters. However, let's also see how the country fared in terms of internal and external peace and security.

Before PM Modi assumed power, India was a victim of hundreds of terror attacks in the country. We remember the 2008 Mumbai terror attacks called the 26/11 attacks in eight locations which lasted for 4 days that resulted in the death of 175 people and 300 injured. In the Jaipur blasts of 2008, 80 people were killed, In the Delhi bomb blasts of 2005, 66 persons were killed and 200 were injured. In 2001, our Parliament was attacked. Ever since 2014, no major terrorist attacks happened on our cities. In the last 9½ years, the country enjoyed peace within the country except in Jammu and Kashmir and in the Naxal affected areas.

Before 2014, India faced continuous infiltrations from Pakistan, ceasefire violations, heavy mortar firing and other threats from Pakistan. Modi Government made it very clear to Pakistan that it will not tolerate cross border terrorism. India took a hawkish approach to

Pakistan and scaled down relations with Pakistan over cross border terrorism. In 2016, India carried out a surgical strike against terrorist infrastructure in Pakistan occupied Kashmir after terrorist attacks on Uri in 2016. Similarly, after the Pulwama terror attack in 2019, India carried out an aerial strike in Balakot.

In the Uri ground strike and the Balakot aerial strike in POK and Pakistan, India, for the first time showed that Pakistan has to pay a price for carrying out terrorist attacks in India. Lack of a proper response to countless terrorist attacks in India, especially the horrendous Mumbai attacks of 2008, made India look like a soft state. That image was changed and India's prestige went up on the global stage.

In the 2017 stand off at Doklam and in the 2020 Eastern Ladakh stand off, India stood up strongly against China's aggressive incursions.

(Please see more details in Chapter on Foreign Relations)

CHAPTER IV

Transformational Schemes

In the last chapter we saw some of the transformational schemes launched by the Modi Government ever since Modi took over as PM in May, 2014.

If we carefully look at these schemes launched in Mission mode, we will see that these programmes have one thing in common. To transform India from the centuries old stagnant mould where people are caught in poverty, backwardness, unhygienic living conditions, unhealthy ambience with no pucca house, no toilet, no clean drinking water, using firewood, cow dung etc. as fuel for cooking, lack of schools and education, lack of medical facilities close by, no electricity, no pucca roads, no skills, unremunerative agriculture dependent on monsoons, lack of irrigation etc. This was the traditional look of life in the villages in rural India. In spite of the efforts of previous Governments, a lot remained to be done. Even in towns and cities in urban India, many of the abovementioned problems existed. So, to lift people up from these subhuman conditions, a farsighted, visionary approach to progress and development was required and what Modi and his team did was exactly that. Where the Swachh Bharat Abhiyan addressed the issue of cleanliness and open defecation by building toilets, PM Awas Yojana Urban and Gramin addressed the lack of housing of crores of families in Urban and rural India. The Jal Jeevan Mission addressed a very fundamental need of the population, clean drinking water. Lack of clean drinking water affected the health of crores of people especially children resulting in life-threatening diseases. The Ujjwala Yojana was focused on addressing the health of women specially and also for ease of living conditions of people in general. Jan Dhan Accounts brought the unbanked people for the first time to the banking system thereby integrating the poor people especially in the rural areas to the modern financial system where they keep their savings as well as avail of credit facilities for emergent needs.

Ayushman Bharat Scheme

Pradhan Mantri Jan Arogya Yojana under Ayushman Bharat is the largest health assurance Scheme in the World. This Scheme aims to provide a health cover of Rs.5 lakhs per family per year for secondary and tertiary care hospitalisation in public and private empanelled hospitals in India to over 12 crore poor and vulnerable families covering over 55 crore beneficiaries.(Why these two figures? Please note 12 crore families. Any member of the family needing hospitalisation can avail of this facility.) This scheme covers the bottom 40% of the Indian population. This Scheme was launched in 2018. The households covered are based on the deprivation and occupational criteria of Socio-economic Caste Census of 2011 for rural and urban areas. It covers up to 3 days of pre-hospitalisation and 15 days of post hospitalisation expenses including diagnostics and medicines. A beneficiary can visit any empanelled hospital to avail cashless treatment.

As on 4 January 2023, 21.9 crore beneficiaries have been verified under PM-JAY. Approximately 4.3 crore hospital admissions costing Rs.50, 409 crore have been authorised under the Scheme through a network of 26, 055 hospitals as per the Economic Survey 2022-23.

Health and Wellness Centres

In February 2018, Government of India announced the creation of 1, 54, 000 Health and Wellness Centres by transforming the existing Sub-centres and Primary Health Centres. These Centres are to deliver Comprehensive Primary Health Care bringing Healthcare closer to the homes of people. "Health and Wellness Centres are envisaged to deliver an expanded range of services to the entire population in their area expanding access, universality and equity close to the Community"(mha.gov.in)

As on 31 Dec 2022, 1, 54, 070 Health and Wellness Centres were operationalised across the country with more than 135 crore cumulative footfall. Under the E-Sanjeevani teleconsultation platform, more than 9.3 crore teleconsultations have been provided through functional HWCs at 15, 465 Hubs and 1, 12, 987 spokes across the country.

Ayushman Bharat Digital Mission

Ayushman Bharat Digital Mission aims at creating a secure online platform that will enable access and exchange of health records of citizens with their consent through services such as issuances of Health ID, Healthcare Professionals Registry, Health Facility Registry and Health Records.

As on 10 Jan 2023, Ayushman Bharat Health Account created 31, 11, 96, 965 Accounts.

Pradhan Mantri Jeevan Jyoti Bima Yojana

Launched in 2015, Pradhan Mantri Jeevan Jyoti Bima Yojana is a one year Life Insurance Scheme giving Life Insurance cover of Rs. 2, 00, 000 at a premium of Re 1 a day(Rs.365 per annum) for people from the age of 18-50.This is renewable from year to year covering life.

It may be recalled that in India, a vast segment of the population, especially the poor and the underprivileged sections of the Society did not have access to insurance cover. These sections used to suffer a heavy blow in the event of any mishap to the family bread winner. This Scheme gives hope to such segments of the population. Till February 2022, 9.27 crore people were enrolled in this Scheme.

Pradhan Mantri Suraksha Bima Yojana

The Pradhan Mantri Suraksha Bima Yojana gives insurance cover of Rs.2 lakhs at a premium of only Re 1 a month and offers a comprehensive cover of Rs.2 lakhs in case of total disability.

As of 23 Feb 2022, 17 crore 74 lakh people have enrolled in PM Suraksha Bima Yojana.

Pradhan Mantri Fasal Bima Yojana

While we are on Insurance coverage, PM Fasal Bima Yojana may be recalled.(Please see more details in Chapter X on Agriculture and Farmer's Welfare). PMFBY was launched from kharif 2016 with the aim to support production in agriculture by giving comprehensive risk cover for crops of farmers against natural risks from pre-sowing to post harvest stage.

As of October 2023, 8 crore policies have been distributed.

29.19 crore farmer applications have insured their crops since 2016. More than Rs.95, 000 crore worth of claims have been provided to farmers since the launch of the Scheme in 2016 against a premium of Rs.17, 000 crore paid by them. The premium is 2% for all kharif and Oilseed crops, 1.5% for Rabi Food and Oilseed crops and 5% for Annual Commercial Horticultural Crops.

Pradhan Mantri Garib Kalyan Yojana

Pradhan Mantri Garib Kalyan Yojana is a scheme to supply free food grains to the poor.

This scheme, initially launched during Covid-19 pandemic and the lockdown during April-June 2020, has now been extended for 5 years.

Under this scheme, the Central Government provides 5 kg of free food grains per month per person and also 1 kg of dal to each family holding a ration card. This is the largest food security program in the world. This scheme benefits over 80 crore people. Over Rs 2 lakh crore provision has been made in the budget 2023 for the scheme. This is in addition to the subsidised (Rs.2-3 per kg) ration provided under the National Food Security Act to families covered under the Public Distribution System. Under the NFSA, 35 kg food grain is provided under Antyodaya Anna Yojana per household per month at Rs.2-3 per kg and an additional 5 kgs of per person for Priority Households. Identification of beneficiaries /households under NFSA is being done by respective state/UT Government.

PM SVANidhi

Ministry of Housing and urban Affairs launched a Scheme in 2020 to empower Street Vendors for their economic development. Under this Scheme a collateral free loan of up to Rs 10, 000 is extended to street vendors for a one year tenure with the proviso for 7% interest subsidy and cashback offers. On repayment of the loan, the beneficiaries can avail of the loan again. Over 60 lakh street vendors in urban areas have been sanctioned loans amounting to Rs 11, 123.60 crores under this Scheme.Most of these beneficiaries have gone in for second and third time loans after repayment of their loans. This is a highly successful Scheme of Modi Government.

(pmsvanidhi.mohua.gov.in)

PM Vishwakarma Kaushal Samman Yojana

On the 77th independence Day, PM Modi announced a Scheme for support of traditional artisans and craftsmen, small business owners and workers. The Scheme was launched on 17 September 2023 with a budget of Rs 13, 000 to 15, 000 crore. The Scheme will offer financial assistance and training to the beneficiaries to modernise their products and give them market access and brand building.

(pmvishvakarmayojana.com)

One Nation One Ration Card

This is a Scheme launched by the Modi Government for the nationwide portability of ration cards under the National Food Security Act. Under this, all eligible ration card holders/beneficiaries can collect their ration food grains from anywhere in the country. This technology enabled Scheme is remarkably transformative that integrates the country and helps lakhs of migrant labour who travels to different parts of the country in search of jobs and livelihood. Started in August 2019, all States and UTs have implemented the Scheme.

24 x7 Electricity supply

Modi Government has set March 2025 as the deadline for 24x7 electricity across the country. Under the Pradhan Mantri Sahaj Bijli Har Ghar Yojana launched in October 2017, Union Government started on the ambitious goal of providing last mile connectivity and electricity connections to all the unelectrified households in the country. India is very close to achieving this target.

Our peak power demand has gone up from 1,36,000 MW in 2014 to 2,34,000 MW in 2024, according to Minister for Power, Shri R.K.Singh. About 1,90,000 MW capacity has been added during Modi Government's time. (Economic times dated 12 February 2024)

CHAPTER V

Infrastructure Development

We know that high quality infrastructure is a fundamental pre-requisite for a country's development. Lack of roads, per se and poor quality of roads where it exists have been a major problem that India faced.

Ever since the Modi Government came to power, development of best quality infrastructure has been a priority for the Government. India saw unprecedented growth in development of infrastructure in the roads and highways sector, ports, airports, national waterways, etc. in the last 9 years and 8 months.

India added nearly the same length of rural roads (3, 48, 000 km) and half the length of National Highways (46, 000 km) in the last 8 years compared to that we had in 70 years before that. (3, 81, 000 km and 97, 000 km).

India had a total of 97, 830 km of National Highways in 2014-15 which has been expanded to 145, 155 km by March 2023. From building 12.1 km per day of roads in 2014-15, the nation is seeing 28.06 km of roads being constructed everyday in 2021-22.

PM Modi's relentless push for infrastructure upgrade to boost the economy has led to phenomenal addition of 50, 000 kms of National Highways, the country's arteries, in the last 9 years.

Roads and Highways play a crucial role in a nation's economy. Road transport is crucial for economic and social development. It is a lifeline for the defence sector and also for making available goods and services throughout the country. It is estimated that 85% of passenger and 70% of goods traffic is carried by roads every year.

As a part of the Bharatmala Pariyojana, India's longest Expressway, 1386 km long Deli-Mumbai expressway is being developed. Delhi-Dausa sector of the expressway has already been dedicated to the nation by PM Modi.

Rural Roads

A total of 6, 45, 605 km road length has been sanctioned under new connectivity and upgradation components under PMGSY-1(Prime Minister Gramin Sadak Yojana-1) out of which 6, 13, 030 km road length has been completed since inception in 2001. 99% of targeted habitations have been provided all weather connectivity as on 10.3.2021.

PMGSY-II was launched in 2013 to upgrade 50, 000 km in various states as a special programme for consolidation of existing Rural Road Network to improve its efficiency not only for transportation but also as a vehicle of social and economic development. Since it's inception till 10.3.2022, 49, 885 km road length has been sanctioned and 46, 468 km road length has been completed under PMGSY-II.

In 2016, Road connectivity Project for Left Wing Extremism Affected Areas (RCPLWEA) for construction/ upgradation of strategically important roads was launched as a special vertical under PMGSY. Since inception, till 10.3.2022, 10, 231 km road length has been sanctioned and 5, 310 km road length has been completed under RCPLWEA.

In the year 2019, Government launched PMGSY III for consolidation of 1, 25, 000 km through Routes and Major Rural Links connecting habitations to Gramin Agricultural Markets, Higher Secondary Schools and Hospitals. Since inception, till 10.3.2022, 77, 129 km, road length has been sanctioned and 29, 773 km road length completed under PMGSY-III.

(Based on information given by MOS Rural Development on 15.3.2022. (pib.gov.in).

Railways

Massive transformational changes have been brought in the Railways in the last 9 ½ years. Conversion to broad-gauge, electrification of lines, manufacturing of rolling stock, manufacturing and introduction of New Vande Bharat Express trains of high speed, increase in passenger and freight traffic, modernisation of the entire Railways, new lines in border areas and North East, retiring of the corrupt from the Railways have been the hallmark of the Indian Railways these years.

Indian Railways recorded the highest ever earnings of Rs. 2.31 lakh crore from freight and passenger segment in 2022-23 which is 28% more than the previous year. It exceeded the revised estimate of Rs. 2.29 lakh more. It further improved to Rs 2, 44, 590 in 2023-24 as per the budget presented on 1 Feb 2024.

90% of Rail network electrified from 600 km to 6, 000 km in 9 ½ years. As of September 2023, 34 semi high speed Vande Bharat Express and 4 Tejas Express trains are operational.

The Railways operate 13, 523 passenger trains , 9, 146 freight trains daily. The Indian Railways has loaded 1, 512 MT during 2022-23 compared to 1, 418 MT during 2021-22. This is the highest ever loading in a financial year. Vision 2024 has been envisaged to achieve targets of 2, 024 MT in loading by 2024.

Average daily track laying is 14.4 kms per day, the highest ever.

785 electric locomotives produced (Manufactured) in 2022-23.

6, 427 stations (98.8% of total stations) have been equipped with electric/electronic signalling interlocking system up to 31.5.2021. 30 freight terminals were created in 2022-23.

Budget allocation for FY-23 for Railways is $29 Billion (Rs 2.40 lakh crore)

Indian Railways has made sustained efforts to improve the service delivery at competitive prices.

Indian Railways is the 4th largest rail freight carrier in the world. Indian Railways is the single largest employer in India. During April-November 2022-23, Indian Railways carried over 4.184 billion passengers.

(https://indianrailways.gov.in)

Metro Rail Network

A Metro revolution is happening in the country with the Metro Rail Network expanding at an unprecedented speed in the last 9 ½ years. From 5 Metro Networks in 2014, the Network has expanded to 20.

Metro Rail provides the fastest and comfortable mobility in the Urban Areas where explosive population growth and lack of proportionate public road transport result in traffic congestion and chaos.

As of November 2023, India has 895 kms of operational Metro line length in 20 cities compared to 248 km of metro line in 2014. The metro ridership is 1 crore a day.

Airports

There were only 74 Airports in the country when the Modi Government took over in 2014. By March, 2023, Government added 74 more airports/heliports/water aerodromes. Government plans to take it to 220 in the coming years.

Air travel which was only limited to a few till the Modi Government assumed power, is within the reach of the common man now.

The total number of domestic passengers in 2014 was 60 million which more than doubled to 143 million in 2020. International passengers increased from 43 million to 64 million in the last 9 ½ years. No of Aircrafts have increased from 400 in 2014 to 723 in 2023 despite the impact of Covid 19 pandemic.

In the last 9 ½ years, 11 more Greenfield airports have been operationalised.

No of Flying Training Organisations increased from 29 to 35 with 54 bases which will increase to 63 by 2023.

UDAN Scheme

Modi Government launched the Ministry of Civil Aviation's flagship programme Regional Connectivity Scheme, UDAN (Ude Desh Ka Nagrik) in October 2016, and the first flight was launched by the PM on 27 April 2017. The objective of the Scheme is to enable the Common man to use Air travel with an enhanced Aviation Infrastructure and air connectivity in Tier II and Tier III cities. 68 underserved/unserved destinations including 58 airports, 8 Heliports and 2 water Aerodromes have been connected under UDAN Scheme.

More than 1 crore passengers have availed the benefits of the Scheme till August 2022. The Scheme offers cheaper air travel under a Regional Connectivity Fund through a levy on certain domestic flights.(pib.gov.in Press Release dated 07 Jun 2023)

Ports

India has a 7500 Km long coastline and 14, 500 Km of potentially navigable Waterways. 12 major and 200 non-major ports located along the Western and Eastern Coastlines are responsible for 90% of India's trade by volume and 70% by value.

Maritime Transport is a critical infrastructure for the country's economy. To meet the ever increasing trade, both imports and exports, Modi Government has been focussed on expansion of Port capacity, Operational efficiencies through mechanisation, digitisation and process simplification. Over the last 9 ½ years, the installed capacity and cargo handled by the Major Ports have increased considerably. The average turnaround time and average output per ship berth day have also improved tremendously.

As per studies by Ministry of Shipping, cargo traffic is expected to be 2, 500 million metric tonnes per annum. A roadmap to increase the port capacity to 3, 300 MMTPA by 2025 has been prepared. This includes improvement of operational efficiency, capacity expansion and new port development.

Cargo Handled by Ports in India

2014 – 972.46 MMTA

2022 – 1323.8 MMTA

This is 70% of trade by value and 95% by volume across the country.

Average turn around time across major ports in India in 2022 was 2.22 days. This is compared to 3.84 days in 2014. The fleet of ships sailing under the Indian flag has expanded from 1250 in 2014 to 1526 by 2023. India's major ports handled highest ever cargo at 795 MMTA in 2022-23.

Inland Waterways

Number of National Waterways developed has gone up from 5 in 2014 to 111 in 2022. For Waterways development, investment went up from Rs. 152 crores to 416.87 crores. Multinational Terminals on National Waterways increased from 1 to 4 from 2014 to 2022. Total Terminals went up from 15 in 2014 to 21 in 2022. Inland water cargo from 30.40 MMT to 108.79 MMTA.

Ganga Vilas Cruise

PM Modi inaugurated on 13 Jan 2023, the country's longest river cruise between Varanasi and Dibrugarh (Assam) covering a distance of 3, 200 km in 50 days.

The ship would pass through the rivers of India and Bangladesh and stop at 50 architecturally important places including world heritage sites. It is a luxury river cruise vessel

(pib.gov.in)

CHAPTER VI

India 5th Largest Economy in the World

India became a $1 trillion economy in 60 years. In 2014 when Modi took over, India was a 1.8 trillion dollar economy. India now is a 3.7 trillion dollar economy and the 5th largest economy in the world surpassing the U.K. who ruled over us for 300 years. In the last 9 ½ years, India became an economic powerhouse from a fragile 5 during the UPA era. This is a phenomenal change. This rapid economic expansion taking place in India is getting the attention of the whole world. Our per capita income was Rs. 78, 000 in 2014 and is Rs. 1, 15, 000 now. ($2610) (Forbes India dated Nov. 23, 2023.)

Our exports were worth $200 billion in 2014 and reached 781.4 billion in 2023.

Our Foreign Exchange Reserves as on 17th Nov. 23 was $ 595 billion compared to $303 billion in 2014.

Our FDI Inflows was $299 billion in 2014. In the 9 ½ years of Modi era since 2014, it is $596 billion.

Bank accounts of Indians cover 98% of the population in 2023 compared to 35% in 2014.

IT Returns filed in 2023-24 were 9.37 crores compared to 3.8 crores in 2014.

India's Defence Exports are worth Rs.16, 000cr now compared to Rs. 1, 000cr in 2014.

India's bank credit stand at Rs.26, 39, 440 crores in 2023 (RBI.org).

India's economic growth in the FY-22-23 was 7.2% as per RBI (RBI.org).World Bank reported that "despite significant global challenges, India was one of the fastest growing economies in FY 2022-23 at 7.2%" (worldbank.org)

It may be mentioned here that the World Economy faced unprecedented challenges from 2020 to 2022 due to Covid 19 pandemic that disrupted normal economic activities. This situation was further compounded by the Russia-Ukraine war that started in February 2022 that triggered a sharp jump in commodity prices especially oil, gas, fertilizer and wheat causing rise in overall inflation. Indian economy was not immune to this. During the fiscal2020-21 GDP contracted by 7.3%.

Modi Government's shrewd handling of the pandemic resulted in the economy making an impressive recovery since the second half of 2020-21.India's Real GDP growth was 9.1% in FY 22, 7.2% in FY 23 and is projected to be 7.3% in FY24. (Economic Review-Ministry of Finance-The Economic Times dated 31 Jan 2023.)

Unemployment rate declined from 9.8% in the quarter ending Sep 2021 to 7.2% in quarter ending Sep 2022, i.e in one year.

India's total food grains production for 2021-22 was 315.7 million tonnes compared to 252 million tonnes in 2014-15.

India's milk production increased by 4% in 2022-23 at 230.58 million tonnes. Egg output increased by 7% to 138.38 billion. Meat production rose by 5% to 9.77 million tonnes (statement by Union Fisheries and Animal Husbandry and Dairying Minister Parshotham Rupala (Economic Times 27th Nov 2023).

Capital Expenditure has been increasing at a scorching pace under the Modi Government. It increased from 1.8 lakh crore in 2018 to Rs 9, 50, 246 crore in FY 24(RE). Private Investment also increased significantly to 3.3 lakh crore in 2022-23 from Rs. 2.8 lakh crore in FY2020.(Economic Survey 2022-23 and Budget 2024 https:// www.indiabudget.gov.in)

World's top 10 countries by GDP(US $ Billions)- Forbes.India.com 23/11/23

1. USA-26, 954
2. China-17, 786
3. Germany-4, 430
4. Japan-4, 231
5. India-3730
6. U.K.-3332
7. France-3052
8. Italy-2190
9. Brazil-2132
10. Canada-2122

India's economy is diverse with swift growth fuelled by key sectors such as Information Technology, services, agriculture and manufacturing.

India's economy has some unique advantages like having a huge domestic market, a youthful and technologically adept labour force and an expanding middle class.

Indian economy grew by 7.6% in the second quarter of FY 2023-24.(pib, gov.in)

Direct Tax Collections in FY 23 was 8.7 lakh crores from 5.4 lakh crores in FY 19. GST Collections went up from 7.8 lakh crore in 2019 to 11.9 lakh crore in FY 23. From a dip in Direct Tax to GDP from 2008 to 2014 from 6 to 5.5 %, now the ratio has gone up to 6% even after a reduction in Corporate Tax in 2019.

Industry contributes 30% of the GVA of the economy employing 12.1 crore people. The eight core industries of coal, fertilisers, cement, steel, electricity, refinery products, crude oil and natural gas saw steady growth over the year.(Economic Survey 2022-23)

Electronics industry is seeing significant growth driven by manufacture of mobile phones, consumer electronics and industrial electronics. The domestic electronics industry was valued at US$118 billion in FY20.India aims to reach US$300 billion in manufacturing and US$ 120 billion in exports by FY 26.

(Economic Survey 2022-23)

CHAPTER VII

Health

Narendra Modi Government gave top most priority to the Health Sector making the Healthcare future ready. It brought a paradigm shift in approach from the treatment of diseases to the wellness of people.

Government's focus was on making the healthcare accessible and affordable. Major initiatives by the government helped in significant improvement in the Health indicators in the last 9 ½ years.

Maternal Mortality Ratio (MMR)in 2014 was 130 per lakh and in 2022, it was 97 per lakh.

Infant Mortality Ratio was 39 in 2014 and 28 in 2022.

Neo-Natal Mortality Ratio (NMR) and under 5 Mortality Ratio(U5MR) was 26 in 2014 and 20 per live births and 45 in 2014 and 32 in 2020 respectively.(pib.gov.in 23 Dec 2022)

Govt launched major health Schemes like the National Health Mission(NHM), Ayushman Bharat-Pradhan Mantri Jan Arogya Yojana, Pradhan Mantri Ayushman Bharat Health Infrastructure Mission (PM-ABHIM), establishment of New Medical Colleges,

Pradhan Mantri Swasthya Suraksha Yojana and many other Schemes.(pib.gov.in 23 Dec 2022)

Total Funds released from 2006-7 to 2013-14 for the Health Sector was Rs 1, 59, 832 crore whereas from 2014-15 to 2021-22, it was Rs 4, 27, 501 crores.

In 2014, there were 8 AIIMS in the country, Under the Modi Government, 15 new AIIMS have been established in different parts of the country taking the total to 23.

Mission Indradhanush

Mission Indradhanush was launched in December 2014, to increase immunisation of children and pregnant women against 8 life threatening diseases like diphtheria, whooping cough, haemophilus influenza type B causing pneumonia and meningitis, tetanus, polio, tuberculosis, measles and hepatitis B in the entire country.

(pib.gov.in 23 DEC 2022)

Ayushman Bharat Yojana

Ayushman Bharat Yojana is the world's largest health assurance Scheme.(Please see more details in Chapter IV under Transformational Schemes)

MBBS seats

There has been a significant increase in the number of medical education seats in the country. Over 35, 000 undergraduate seats have been added. Total number of MBBS seats increased from 51, 348 in 2014 to 88, 120 seats in 2021, 72% increase.

PG Seats have seen a phenomenal growth. There are 55, 595 PG seats in the country including DNB and Diploma Courses in other specialities. This is a 78% increase compared to 2014.

The increase in seats will bring India achieve the World Bank prescribed ratio of 1 Doctor for 1, 000 persons.

Medical Colleges

Close to 179 new medical colleges opened across the country between 2014 and 2020. (https:pib.gov.in Press Release).

The Central Government has approved more than Rs 25,000 crores for the establishment of new medical colleges.

Taking medical education to the most backward areas

The Government has approved establishment of 157 medical colleges attached to existing District hospitals. These districts include some of the remotest and economically backward districts. This helps in making medical education more accessible. Many Districts will be getting their first medical college after more than 7 decades of Independence.

These new Medical colleges will add more than 15, 000 medical seats collectively.

National Medical Commission

In a major reform in the Healthcare Sector, the Government replaced the Medical Council of India (which functioned in a controversial manner), with a 33 member National Medical Commission to ensure greater transparency and accountability in medical education.

Pradhan Mantri Jan Aushudhi Pariyojana

PM Janaushudhi Scheme was launched by the PM in 2015 to provide generic drugs at cheaper prices ensuring quality and efficacy.

Prices of Janaushudhi medicines are 50%-90% cheaper than that of branded medicines i.e. the open market.

Medicines are procured from WHO – Good Manufacturing Practice certified suppliers for ensuring quality of products. Each batch of drugs is tested at laboratories accredited by National Accreditation Board for Testing.

As on 30.11.2023, there are 10, 001 kendras in the country.

(https://janaushadi.gov.in)

CHAPTER VIII

Covid 19 – Pandemic

India and the whole world faced the biggest challenge of the century with the onset of Covid 19 pandemic in early January 2020. This was the biggest challenge to Modi also as the Prime Minister.

The life threatening Corona virus turned the normal life upside down. The rapidly transmitting infectious disease which started in Wuhan, China in end December, 2019 reached India through a student returning from China to Kerala on Jan 30, 2020.

Ever since the Covid 19 case was first reported in China, Prime Minister's office got into action. From January 2020 itself, Modi was personally overseeing the situation and ensured immediate Government response. ICMR and NCDC (National Centre for Disease Control) started tracking returnees from China and monitoring Covid 19 testing. Even before WHO declared Covid 19 as a pandemic, India already had put in place institutional mechanisms. Public health experts and medical professionals and the Government machinery were charting a strategy to face the challenge.

The Government of India constituted 11 empowered Groups on 29 March 2020 on different aspects of Covid

19 management in the country to take informed decisions on medical emergency planning, availability of hospitals, isolation and quarantine facilities, disease surveillance and testing, availability of essential medical equipment, augmenting human resources, supply chain and logistics management and communication and public awareness.

The Government started screening at airports, creating awareness of Covid 19 and its symptoms, building additional testing infrastructures and arranging isolation facilities across the country to reduce transmissions. The entire health infrastructure was put on 24 hours alert and service.

The Modi Government, in a unique governance style, took a "whole of Government" approach to tackle the crisis. India was one of the first countries to evacuate its citizens from China.

Government started screening passengers at all entry points and quarantined those who tested positive; arrangements were made to ensure adequate supply of essential items needed for Covid 19 treatment.

National Lockdown

As the Covid 19 situation deteriorated and cases started rising, Modi Government imposed a complete national lockdown from March 25, 2020 to control the spread of infection. This was a difficult decision for Modi.

PM Modi addressed the nation and told the citizens to brace up to face the challenge. He advised citizens to keep "do gaj ki doori" to emphasize on social distancing.

Modi reached out to various sections of the society through religious leaders, healthcare professionals, radio jockeys, journalists, etc., to create awareness about Covid 19. Government used mobile phones through SMS and voice messages, radio announcements, TV announcements, by putting bill boards at all public places, using social influencers like actors to spread the precautions that the citizens should take to prevent the spread of Covid 19.These steps were using of N-95 masks, social distancing, frequent washing of hands, avoiding public places as much as possible and to seek medical assistance in case Covid 19 symptoms.

The lockdown was extended and lasted 68 days. India timed the lockdown at the appropriate time when there were only a few cases. The Global response to arrest transmission was lockdown.

Though the lockdown resulted in disruption of everyday life and also economic activities, Modi's decision was the most appropriate at that time of the disease spread. Modi's call to light a lamp and compliment healthcare workers by playing utensils (thali) were mocked by some but it helped in spreading awareness. Further it raised hope, optimism and positivity in people.

Atmanirbhar Bharat

When the Covid pandemic started, India was in shortfall of medical supplies and infrastructure like testing facilities, N-95 masks, PPE kits for health workers, ventilators, hospital beds, liquid oxygen, etc. Modi Government geared up the government and private production facilities to fight Covid 19 in a few months time.

In March 2020, there were only 52 labs to test the disease. With the untiring efforts of various agencies, 1, 364 RT-PCR testing facilities were brought up in a few months. By 2022, there were 3, 000 testing facilities in the country. Rapid testing kits were also developed by public and private sector bodies. Most public hospitals now have RT-PCR testing facility.

In 2020, there was a huge shortage of N-95 masks and PPE kits. In the initial stage, our healthcare workers did not have PPE kits to treat the Covid patients. There was a global shortage. PM Modi oversaw that Ministry of Textiles through industry bodies approached manufacturers to produce PPE kits and N-95 masks. The Government offered support and technical knowledge and more that 600 domestic manufacturers started producing PPE kits.

When the pandemic began, there were only 17, 850 ventilators in public hospitals. In April, 2020, Modi Government placed orders for 50, 000 ventilators. These were paid for entirely by the Government through PM Cares Funds and distributed to state Governments for public hospitals. A design for indigenous ventilator was created and the public sector Bharat Electronics was asked to manufacture and supply 30, 000 ventilators.

Modi Government's coordinated efforts to push for enhanced production of ventilators, PPE kits, N-95 masks and expansion of testing capacity are a remarkable success in achieving self-sufficiency and the idea of Atma Nirbhar Bharat.

The Second Covid 19 Wave

In April-May, 2021, the highly transmissible Delta Variant created havoc the world over and India was no exception. The entire medical infrastructure was put to test as the cases roses exponentially.

Oxygen Shortage

The Delta wave led to the need for large scale hospitalisation where patients needed oxygen to survive. The requirement of oxygen went up so much that the country faced a crisis situation.

Limited oxygen production and the fact that production was concentrated in East India was one problem. Another problem was oxygen delivery to the entire country. Shortage of cryogenic tankers for transporting liquid oxygen was a third problem.

Modi is reputed to find novel solutions in crunch situations. Modi Government requisitioned the services of the Indian Railways, Indian Air Force and the Indian Navy for assistance in Oxygen transportation. The Railways launched special oxygen express trains for delivering liquid oxygen to different parts of the country. The Air Force transported empty cryogenic tankers within the country and from abroad. Production of medical oxygen was increased in all production centres.

Shortage of hospital beds and medicines were also addressed by the Modi Government. By 2021, the number of isolation beds and ICU beds were revamped up 155 times and 40 times respectively compared to 2020.

Makeshift facilities and field hospitals were established in Delhi by the Central Government. One example was the 10, 000 bed Sardar Patel Covid 19 care centre in Delhi. More than 2100 beds were provided by the Central Government Hospitals for Covid 19 patients. The Armed Forces Medical Service, DRDO, Defence PSUs and Cantonment Boards came together to increase the availability of hospital beds. DRDO set up special Covid 19 facilities across the country. 4, 000 Railway coaches were converted into Covid 19 care facilities.

COVID 19 VACCINATION

The Covid 19 vaccination programme was a remarkable case study of the vision, planning and execution of a mass programme by the Modi Government. PM Modi's extraordinary skills in vision and execution of huge national level programmes could be seen in the vaccination success of the country.

The Covid 19 Vaccination Mission was launched in November 2020 for vaccination research and development. Modi Government gave Rs. 900 crore for these efforts to various agencies. ICMR supported vaccine manufacturers in vaccine research and for clinical trials.

Bharat Biotech and ICMR jointly developed Covaxin, a major achievement for the country. The Department of Biotechnology facilitated technology transfer to various companies like Haltkaine

Biopharmaceutical Corporation Ltd., Indian Immunological Limited and Hester Bio Sciences.

Support was given to vaccine manufacturers, Serum Institute of India and Bharat Biotech by giving advance payments and orders. 100% advance payments of Rs. 1, 732 crores and Rs. 787 crores were released to SII and Bharat Biotech respectively.

As of 31 December 2021, 145 crore vaccines were administered. India administered more vaccine doses than that of many continents put together. Over 90% of the population got at least one dose. About 60% got both doses. (www.theHindu.com/coronavirus). Many states and Union Territories have achieved 100% coverage. It took 85 days to administer the first 10 crore doses. Later the pace of vaccination went up to 10 crore doses in a fortnight. In 9 months, 100 crore milestone was reached.

In the vaccination drive, the biggest in the world, Modi Government used digital technology by creating Arogya Sethu App (Co-win) App, to register and locate the nearest vaccination centres to get vaccinated and also to get the vaccination certificates. It was a very smart use of the Digital Technology during the Covid Emergency. The Co-Win App was especially useful wherever vaccination certificate were to be shown like for air travel.

In the "Whole of Government" approach, post offices, schools, Anganwadis and public institutions were involved in widening the vaccine drive.

As on 31 January 2024, 220, 67, 85, 749 total vaccinations were given in the country.(mohfw.gov.in)

As per Worldometer's figures on 1 Feb 2024, close to 4.5 crore Indians were infected by Covid 19 and

5, 33, 448 deaths were reported. India fared better than US and UK in cases per million citizens. In India, there were 32, 010 cases per million citizens whereas in the US there were 3, 31, 066 cases per million and in the UK 3, 63, 307. The number of deaths per million in India were 379, lower than that of 3570 in the US and 3389 in the UK.(worldometers.info)

The great leadership that PM Modi gave to the country and to our health care professionals to manage the deadliest pandemic of a hundred years deserves appreciation of the highest level. In the face of a huge crisis with pessimism about India's capability to handle the crisis, Prime Minister stood steadfastly to save our countrymen from the jaws of death.

In a very typical Modi style, India used the crisis for "Vaccine Maitri" with a large number of developing countries who were in a dire situation for want of vaccines. India sent vaccines to 94 countries and two UN entities. (https://pib.gov.in press release page .aspx.PRID1715649).

(static.pib.gov.in press release dated December 24, 2021)

CHAPTER IX

Education

The Modi Government has initiated major transformational changes in the Education Sector with a focus on primary, higher and Medical Education.

Modi Government established two colleges every day and one University every week ever since coming to power. There were 723 Universities in 2014 and 1100 universities in 2023. There were 16 IITs in 2014 and 23 in 2023. There were 13 IIMs in 2014 and 20 in 2023. A new IIT and IIM has been opened every year since 2014. There were 9 IIITs (Indian Institute of Information Technology) in 2014 and 25 in 2022. There were 7 AIIMS in 2014 and 22 in 2023. There were 387 medical colleges in 2014 and 660 in 2023.(myGov.in)

Total enrolments in higher education increased to 4.33 crore in 2021 compared to 3.42 crore in 2014-15, a 26.5% increase.(All India Survey on Higher Education.)

Because of the sharp increase in the number of Higher Education Institutions, the number of students in higher education has gone up significantly.

22 new universities have been set up in the North East and Ladakh has got its first ever Central University,

first ever Forensic University and Rail and Transport university also established.

71 Indian universities have made it to the World University rankings, up from 63 last year.

Primary Education

Major focus has been laid on improving the primary education system. Emphasis is on preparing the students for 21st century. Gross enrolments of girls has increased in higher education by 18% from 2015 to 2020 thereby giving a fillip to PM's vision of Beti Bachao Beti Padhao.

In FY 2022, a total of 26.5 crore children were enrolled in schools. During the year, 1 crore children enrolled in pre-primary, 12.2 crore in primary, 6.7 crore in upper primary, 3.9 crore in secondary and 2.9 crore in higher secondary.(Economic Survey 2022-23)

School drop-out rates at all levels have seen a steady decline in recent years. From 4.7% in primary, 3.1% in Upper primary, 14.5% in Secondary in 2013-14, the drop out rate decreased to 1.5% in primary, 3.0% in Upper primary and 12.6% in Secondary schools.(Economic Survey 2022-23)

Pupil-teacher ratio has improved, raising quality of education. School infrastructure is being upgraded. 8,700 Atal Tinkering labs have been set up since 2015. Amenities like electricity, libraries, girls toilets, medical check-up in schools have been ramped up significantly. In 2013, only 55% of the schools had electricity. It increased to 83% in 2020. In 2014, only 69% schools had library/reading room. It increased to 84% in 2020.(Economic Survey 2022-23)

In 2013, only 36% of schools had hand wash facility. By 2020 it was covered to 90%. In 2013, only 89% of schools had girls toilets but by 2020, it was covered to 97%. 61% of schools had medical check-up in a year. It was increased to 82% by 2022.(Economic Survey 2022-23)

Medical Education is being given a big push. MBBS seats increased by 53% from 51, 348 in 2014 to 96, 077 in 2020. Post Graduate Medical Seats increased by 80% from 30, 191 in 2014 to 54, 275 in 2020. (source Narendra Modi.in).

The schemes like Samagra Shiksha, RTE Act, improvement in school infrastructure and facilities, residential hostel buildings, availability of teachers, free textbooks, free uniforms for children, establishment of Kasturba Gandhi Balika Vidyalayas and the PM POSHAN scheme play an important role in enhancing enrolment and retention of children in school.

PM Schools for Rising India

Government of India launched PM Schools for Rising India on 7 September 2022. These schools will be equipped with modern infrastructure and showcase implementation of NEP to emerge as exemplary schools. Under this scheme, 14, 500 PM SHRI schools will be set up.(Economic Survey 2022-23)

Samagra Shiksha Schemes

Under the ICT component of the scheme, on the recommendation of NEP 20, computer literacy and computer enabled learning will be imparted to children. It envisages covering all Government/Govt. aided schools from classes VI to classes XII. Till November 2022, ICT labs have been approved in 1, 20, 614 schools and smart classrooms in 82, 120 schools across the country. (Economic Survey 2022-23)

Skill Development

Modi Govt. set up a Ministry of Skill Development and Entrepreneurship (MSDE) in 2014 and skills India Mission was launched in 2015. This Ministry is tasked with skill development aimed at removal of the disconnect between demand and supply of skilled Manpower by building vocational and technical training, skill upgradation, building new skills for the existing jobs and for the future. NEP 20 also focuses on vocational education and skill development. (Economic Survey 2022-23)

Skill India Mission

Skill India Mission focuses on skilling, re-skilling and up-skilling through short term and long term training programmes. Under the Mission, Government, through 20 Central Ministries/Departments is implementing various skill development schemes like Deen Dayal Upadhyay Grameen Kaushalya Yojana, Rural self-employment Training Institutes (RSETI), Deen Dayal Antyodaya National Urban Livelihood

Mission (DAY-NULM). MSDE is implementing Pradhan Mantri Kaushal Vikas Yojana, Jan Shiksha Sansthan (JSS), National Apprenticeship Promotion scheme (NAPS) and Craftsmen Training Scheme.(Economic Survey 2022-23)(Economic Survey 2022-23)

Under PMKVY (PMKVY2.0), between FY17 and FY23 (as of 5 Jan 2023), 1.1 crore persons have been trained, 83% certified and aout 21.4 lakh placed for jobs. Under PMKVY 3.0, during FY21 to FY23 (as of 5 Jan 2023), 7.4 lakh persons have been trained, 66% certified and 41, 437 placed.(Economic Survey-2022-23)(Economic Survey 2022-23)

PMKVY also provided training to (migrant labourers) affected by Covid 19. This covered 116 districts. 1.3 lakh migrants have been trained / oriented.

Under Jan Shiksha Sansthan Scheme, from FY20 to FY23 (as of 5/1/23), 16.0 lakhs beneficiaries have been trained. Jan Shiksha Sansthan are provided lump sum grants for skills training to non-literate, near-literate and school drop outs up to class XII.(Economic Survey 2022-23)

Under the National Apprenticeship Promotion Scheme, the Government provides financial support to Industrial establishments. Since the launch of the scheme in 2016 as on 31 December 2022, 21.4 lakh apprentices have been engaged by Industries.(Economic survey 2022-23)

Under the Craftsmen Training Scheme, long training in 149 trades through 14, 938 Industrial Training Institutes across the country. Since 2015, 91.7

lakh students have been trained as on 30 October 2022. (msde.gov.in)

Skill India International Network

With an aim to make India a skill Capital of the world, National Skill Development Corporation is set up (NSDC). It will create a network of Skill India International Network involving both Government and Private Institutions. (msde.gov.in)

Beti Bacaho Beti Padhao

This chapter cannot end without a reference to the 'Beti Bachao Beti Padhao' Scheme launched by PM Modi in 2015.

A scheme envisaged to protect the girl child and educate the girl children, PM Modi, in a way replicated the hugely successful Kanya Kelavani Nidhi programme in Gujarat when he was Chief Minister of Gujarat on a National level.

MHRD is setting up 5, 930 schools called Kasturba Gandhi Balika Vidyalayas, residential schools for girls that give girls access to quality education. As per the Annual Status of Education Report Survey, percentage of girls out of school between the ages of 11 and 14 years has shown a steady decline from 10.3 in 2006 to 4.1 in 2018 and to 3.9% in 2021. The ASER survey also shows a rise in girls' enrolment in Government schools with the percentage rising from 70% in 2018 to 73% in 2020.

CHAPTER X

Agriculture and Farmers

Agriculture and its allied sectors like animal husbandry and fisheries is the largest livelihood provider in India especially in the rural areas.

As per the Economic Survey 2022-23, it contributes 18.3% of the Gross Domestic Product of India's Economy.

Modi Government took a slew of measures to augment crop and livestock productivity, to ensure that certainty of returns to the farmers through Minimum Support Price, promote crop diversification, improve market infrastructure by setting up farmer-producer organisations and the setting up of the Agriculture Infrastructure Fund.

The Indian Agriculture Sector has been growing at an average annual growth rate of 4.6% over the last six years. It grew by 3% in 2021-22 and 3.3% in 2020-21.

During the year 2021-22, agricultural exports reached an all time high of $50.2 billion. (Economic Survey 2022-23)

PM-KISAN

Under the Pradhan Mantri Kisan Samman Nidhi (PM_KISAN), an income support of Rs 6, 000 per annum in three equal instalments is provided to all landholding farmers except those excluded under the higher economic status. Money is transferred directly into the bank accounts of beneficiaries under Direct Benefit Transfer. About 11.19 crore farmer families are benefitting under this Scheme. 15th instalment of the PM KISAN scheme was released on 15 November 2023.

(https://pmkisan.gov.in)

PM-KMY(Pradhan Mantri Kisan Maan Dhan Yojana)

This is a Scheme launched by the Modi Government to provide Social Security to all Small and marginal Farmers. Under the Scheme, a pension of Rs 3, 000 will be provided to all eligible farmers. Farmers will have to contribute between Rs 55 to Rs 200 per month in the Pension Fund managed by LIC of India till they reach the retirement age of 60. Government of India makes an equal contribution of the same amount in the Pension Fund. Spouses of the farmers are also eligible to join the Scheme. (pmkmy.gov.in)

PM Fasal Bima Yojana

PMFBY was launched from Kharif 2016 with an aim to support production in agriculture by giving comprehensive risk cover for crops of farmers against unpreventable natural risks from sowing to post harvest stage.

As of October, 2023, 8 crore policies have been distributed.

29.19 crore farmer applications have insured their crops since 2016. More than Rs.95, 000 crore worth of claims have been provided to farmers since the launch of the scheme in 2016 against a premium of Rs.17, 000 crore paid by them. The premium is 2% for all Kharif and Oilseed crops, 1.5% for Annual Commercial Horticulture crops.
(https://pmfby.gov.in)(Economic Survey 2022-23)

MSP 1.5 Times the Cost of Production

One of the long standing woes Indian farmers faced was that they were not getting adequate remunerative return over the cost of production. Modi Government announced in the Union Budget 2018-19 that farmers would be given Minimum Support Price of at least one and a half times the cost of production. Accordingly, the Government has been increasing the MSP for all 22 Kharif, Rabi and other commercial crops with a margin of at least 50% over the all India weighted average cost of production since 2018-19. To achieve self-sufficiency in pulses and oilseeds production, Govt. has fixed higher MSP for pulses and Oilseeds. Thus, there has been a steady increase in the MSP of all crops since 2018-19.(Economic Survey 2022-23)

Cheaper an Enhanced Credit to Farmers

To ensure hassle free credit to farmers, at cheaper rates, the Kisan Credit Scheme was extended by Modi Govt. to fisheries and animal husbandry farmers in 2018-19. As of December 2022, banks issued Kisan Credit

Cards to 3.89 farmers with credit of Rs. 4, 51, 672 crores. As of 17 October, 2022, 1.0 lakh KCCs have been issued to fisheries sector and 9.5 lakh to the animal husbandry sector.

Under the Modified Interest Subvention Scheme, to provide short term credit to farmers, at subsidized rates, a short term loan up to Rs. 3 lakhs is available at 7% annual interest. An additional 3% subvention (Prompt Repayment Incentive) is also given to farmers for timely repayment of loans. Thus, if a farmer repays his loan on time, he gets credit of 4% per annum.

There has been a consistent increase in agriculture credit flow over the years. In 2021-22, there was 13% increase, exceeding the target of 16.5 lakh crore. The target for 2022-23 was 18.5 lakh crore.

Compared to 2014, the increase in Institutional Credit to Agriculture has gone up from 8.5 lakh crore in 2014 to 18.6 lakh crore in 2021-22. (Economic Survey-2022-23)

Improving Productivity

To Improve productivity, State Governments are being assisted by Centre in training in use of agricultural machinery by setting up Custom Hiring Centres.

Organic Farming

For promoting organic farming, two dedicated schemes, Paramparagat Vikas Yojana, Mission Organic Vikas Chain for Development of North Eastern Region have been started since 2015. Financial Assistance of

Rs.50, 000 per hectare for 3 years is provided to the farmers out of which Rs.31, 000 is given as incentive for organic imports, given directly through DBT. As of November 2022, 32, 384 clusters of 20 Hectare size totalling 6.4 lakh hectare area and 16.1 lakh farmers have been covered. In addition, under the Namami Gange programme, 1.2 lakh hectare area has been covered under organic farming. Under special scheme for North East, 1.5 lakh farmers and 1.7 lakh hectares have been covered.

Natural Farming

Under Natural farming (Bharatiya Prakratik Krishi Paddhati) BPKP under PKVY, 4.09 lakh hectare of land have been brought under Natural farming in States.

Agricultural Infrastructure Fund

AIF is a financing facility operated from 2020-21 to 2032-33 for creation of post harvest management infrastructure for warehouses, primary processing units, sorting and grading cold storage projects, etc. Since its inception, Rs.13, 681 crore has been sanctioned covering 18, 133 projects.

Mission for Integrated Development of Horticulture was launched in 2014-15 to promote horticulture covering fruits, vegetables, root and tuber crops, spices, flowers, plantation crops etc. Interventions include improved varieties and quality seeds, incentives for plantation crops cluster development and post-harvest management. In 2021-22, a record production of 342.3

million tonnes of horticultural products was achieved in an area of 28 million hectares.

National Agriculture Market (e-NAM) Scheme.

Modi Government launched the National Agriculture Market (e-NAM) Scheme in 2016 to create an online transparent, competitive bidding system to ensure farmers get remunerative prices for their produce. Under the Scheme, Government provides free software and assistance of Rs75 lakhs per APMC Mandi for related hardware, quality assaying equipment and the creation of infrastructure for cleaning, grading, sorting, packaging etc. As on 31 December 2022, more than 1.7 crore farmers and 2.3 lakh trades have been registered in e-NAM portal.

International Year of Millets

Under India's initiative, the UN General Assembly declared 2023 as the International Year of Millets to promote cultivation and consumption of millets. Millets are high in nutritional value, are climate resilient and align with several UN Sustainable Development Goals. Millets have great potential to generate livelihood, increase farmer's income, ensure food and nutritional security all over the world.

India produces more than 50.9 million tonnes of millet accounting for 80% of Asia's and 20% of global production. Millets require less water to grow.

Government of India notified Millets as Nutri-cereals in 2018 and Under national Food Security

Mission, millets have been introduced to provide nutritional support.

India has more than 500 start-ups working in the millet value chain. Indian Institute of Millets Research has incubated 250 start-ups under Rashtriya Krishi Vikasana Yojana. (Economic Survey 2022-23)

Millets were part of the cuisine served to thousands of international delegates who participated in the G-20 Summit. Major Indian Consumer Products companies like ITC, Nestle have already introduced various millets based food products in the market.

Animal Husbandry, Dairying and Fisheries.

The allied sectors of Indian agriculture like livestock, forestry and logging, fishing and aquaculture are seeing buoyant growth and are potential source of better incomes for farmers.

The livestock sector grew at 7.9% CAGR from 2014-15 to 2020-21 and contributed 30% of Gross Value Addition to agriculture in 2020-21 compared to 24.3% in 2014-15.

Fisheries Sector is growing at 7% since 2016-17 and contributes 6.7% GVA in Agriculture.

The Dairy Sector is the critical component of the livestock sector employing more than 8 crore farmers directly. India ranks 1st in milk production in the world, third in eggs production and eighth in meat production in the world.

Government of India launched the Animal Husbandry Infrastructure Development Fund worth Rs 15, 000 crore I 2020 to improve livestock productivity and disease control. National Animal Disease Control Programme is being implemented to control Foot& Mouth Disease and Brucellosis by completely vaccinating cattle, sheep, goat and pig populations. (Economic Survey 2022-23)

Pradhan Mantri Matsya Sampada Yojana

With a total outlay of Rs 20, 050 crore, the highest ever investment in the fisheries Sector in India is to be implemented over 5 years from FY 21 to FY 25 in all states and UTs.The objective of the Scheme is to drive sustainable and responsible development of the Fisheries Sector helping the socio-economic development of fishers, fish farmers and fish workers. (Economic Survey 2022-23)

Prime Minister Krishi Sinchai Yojana

Modi Government launched the PM Krishi Sinchai Yojana in FY 2015-16 to enhance physical access of water on farm and expand cultivable area under irrigation, improving water use efficiency and water conservation practice. "Har Khet Ko Pani" is one of the components of PM Krishi Sinchai Yojana. (https://static.pib.gov.in)

Mission Amrit Sarovar

PM launched a new initiative under Mission Amrit Sarovar on 24 April 2022. The Mission is aimed at developing and rejuvenating 75 water bodies in each district of the country as a part of the Azadi ka Amrit Mahotsav. A total of 50, 000 Amrit Sarovars are to be develop-ed under the Scheme.

CHAPTER XI

Foreign Policy

In the last 9 years and 8 months, after PM Modi took over as the Prime Minister, India's Foreign Policy achieved a new paradigm, a new enthusiasm and energy, a new spring in it's steps.

Over these years India's profile has gone up internationally as never before. Modi easily established friendships with World leaders, travelled around the globe, won hearts of Indians/PIOs and foreigners alike and in the process showcased a New India to the World.

Modi invited leaders from all neighbouring countries for his swearing -in ceremony. This was simply unprecedented. These leaders attended the function enthusiastically. This gesture put into practice India's policy of neighbourhood First.

From a time when India had to knock at the doors of economic powers for investments and technology, now almost all the countries in the World want to have a presence in India, either to invest in India or seeking investments, trade, tourists, students, our experts and manpower etc. This is a historic change.

How did this change happen?

Undoubtedly, the overall strides India is making in various spheres under PM Modi have a big role to play in this sea change in perception about India. India's economic growth, making it the 5th largest Economy in the world, improvement in ease of doing business in India, India's demographic dividend with 65% of India's population below the age of 35 years, India emerging as an IT and Technology powerhouse extending IT/ITES services to the world, the world looking to India for their manpower needs, India's credentials as the world's largest democracy, India's strong policy framework, Digital Public Infrastructure, India's robust legal/judicial Framework, India's superb management of the deadly Covid-19 pandemic and its success in vaccinating 1.4 billion people using our own homemade vaccines, India's stellar leadership of G-20 Summit etc. had a multiplier effect.

Another important reason is that India is a huge market for world's manufacturers, exporters, business and Industry. India's diaspora of 30 million strength is another driver of this unprecedented, historic interest in India. The fact that some of the biggest Corporations of the world, about 21 of these, like Microsoft, Google, Adobe, IBM, Novartis, Micron Technology etc., are run by India born CEOs act as catalyst.

Think of it !

India is the most populous country in the world at 142, 57, 75, 850 in April 2023 as per UN (UNDESA Policy Board No 153), surpassing China.

India's youth population (below 35 years) is around 65% of the total population i.e. 92.3 crore (923 million) !

Modi Government's big push in the Education Sector resulted in India having 1100 Universities (723 in 2014) and 43, 796 colleges. India's 23 IITs (16 in 2014), 20 IIMs (12 in 2014), 22 (AIIMS) (7 in 2014) and 660 Medical colleges (387 in 2014) churn out top level talent who are in big demand through out the world.

India is an emerging power that no country in the world can ignore. In the last 10 years, India has emerged as a military power to reckon with. Modi Govt.'s big push to the Defence Sector under the Atma Nirbhar Bharat is catapulting India into a major producer of Defence equipments. India has built and commissioned it's own Aircraft carrier (INS Vikrant), India is producing it's own fighter jets (Tejas), it's own Battle tanks (Arjun), Armoured Personnel carriers, Field guns and other military assets and infrastructure that make India to stand up to any powerful enemy.

India is a nuclear power with its own Nuclear Triad. With a strength of close to 1.3 million active personnel (mygov.in), India has the world's second largest military force. India has the third largest defence budget in the world. The Global Fire Power Index report lists it as the fourth most powerful military.

India also has a multi-layer ballistic missile defence system to protect our country. India has its nuclear capable Inter-Continental Ballistic Missiles, Agni V, developed by the Defence Research and Development Organisation of India. India's Agni VI is expected to have a range of 9, 000km to 12, 000 km with a 3 tonne nuclear payload. (www.indiatoday.in)

India is also a Space Power. Under PM Modi's leadership, Indian Space Programme achieved greater heights in the last 9 ½ years. India has indigenous capability to build and launch its own satellites for telecommunications, broadcasting, meteorology, remote sensing programme for application of satellite imagery etc. India has achieved 122 Spacecraft Missions so far including the successful landing of Chandrayan-3 on the South Pole of Moon last year (2023).India also recently launched Aditya L1 Mission to study the Sun which has been successfully placed in the L1 orbit. Earlier India had successfully launched the Mars Orbiter Mission.

India has launched 432 foreign satellites so far and had 6 re-entry Missions.

India has plans to send an astronomer to space and also plans to have a space station by 2035. (www.isro.in)

India's diplomatic presence abroad

As of February 2022, India had 202 operational Indian Missions/Posts abroad covering 141 countries. (mea.gov.in)

Since the Modi Government took over in 2014, 22 new Indian diplomatic Missions/Posts have been established.

The thumb rule in establishing new Missions /Posts abroad is to protect India's national interests, expanding trade and investments, tourism opportunities, political and strategic interests, welfare of Indian nationals and

Persons of Indian Origin, facilitating visa services to the nationals of the host countries, etc.

India extended Rs 90, 348 crore in Grants and loans to various developing countries between 2014 to 2021.US$ 22, 439 million worth of Lines of Credit have been extended to developing countries between 2014-2024. (mea.gov.in)

PM's honest efforts to improve relations with it's neighbours.

Prime Minister Modi brought fresh thinking, ideas and new Initiatives in Foreign Policy. Through his "Neighbourhood First" Policy, vigorous efforts were made for closer ties with neighbouring countries. India could settle its land and maritime boundaries with Bangladesh, connectivity was improved and India maintained close relations with it's top leadership. When a massive earthquake hit Nepal, India was the first responder, immediately rushing help to Nepal. Recently when Sri Lanka faced a grave economic crisis, India extended financial and material help to Sri Lanka.Despite political turmoil within Myanmar, India continued to maintain stable relations with that country. Political changes in Maldives is bringing some challenges to the close relations India had with Maldives. India continued to strengthen relations with Bhutan during the last decade and enjoys very close relations with Bhutan. The Taliban taking over the control of Afghanistan and US's troop withdrawal from there was a new reality India had to deal with. Despite this development, India has been extending humanitarian aid to Afghanistan. India's complex and complicated relations with Pakistan and China will be discussed separately. In spite of the fact that relations with foreign countries is an ever dynamic process and India being a big neighbour will have its own challenges in it's relations with its small neighbours, India honestly tried to improve relations with all its neighbours.

During the Modi era, India developed closer relations with the United States of America. Modi had very good equations with all the three Presidents, Obama, Trump and Biden. India deepened its strategic relations with the US. Us is supplying India with cutting edge defence equipments. Initiative of Critical and Emerging Technologies, the Agreement to co-produce GE-Jet Engines, Deal for India to buy 31 MQ-9B Predator drones, Advanced Domains Defence Dialogue, India-US Acceleration Ecosystem etc., show the Strategic Partnership of India and the US.

India continued to have friendly and stable relations with Canada except for some sore points that cropped up very recently because of the anti-Indian activities of Khalistani activists, terrorists and gangsters based in Canada.

India further strengthened relations with countries like Brazil, Argentina and other countries in Latin America and the Caribbean and Central America.

India continued to have close relations with Russia which is a major supplier of defence equipments to India. India meticulously positioned its relations with Russia after the outbreak of the Ukraine -Russia war despite pressure from the Western countries.

India's traditional friendly relations with Japan, Australia and other countries in East Asia and South East Asia and Oceania further strengthened during PM Modi's premiership.

Our relations with France deepened with France emerging as a key supplier of State-of-the Art defence supplies like Rafael fighter jets.

India's relations with EU and other countries in Europe further strengthened. India continues to have strong relations with the U.K.

India's relations with countries in the Indian Ocean Region, the Eurasian Countries, West Asia and the Gulf countries, North Africa, continued to be friendly and deep. India also has good relations with Iran and Iraq.

India further strengthened its traditionally strong relations with countries in Africa.

With the rising profile of India globally, India is playing a leading role in the United Nations and other International Organisations and other Multilateral Institutions.

Pakistan

After PM Modi took over in 2014, India made it very clear to Pakistan that till the time Pakistan stopped promoting cross border terrorism from Pakistan's soil, normal relations with it would not be possible. It may be mentioned that Modi made an honest effort to repair relations with Pakistan initially. He invited Nawas Sharif alongwith other Heads of states/Governments to his swearing in. He also made an impromptu visit to Lahore in December 2015.

In January 2016, there was a big attack on the Pathankot Army Cantonment by terrorists supported by Pakistan. After this incident, Modi cancelled the planned talks with Pakistan conveying that any dialogue with Pakistan would depend on credible action against militants who were behind the Pathankot attack. Pakistan continued to send terrorists to India. When there was another attack by terrorists on India's military base in Uri on 18 September 2016, killing 19 Indian soldiers, India conducted surgical strikes inside Pakistan Occupied Kashmir on 29 September 2016 targeting terrorist camps. In 2019, India launched air strikes in Balakot in Pakistan against terrorist camps after a terrorist strike in Pulwama on an Indian military convoy. Pakistan retaliated by launching airstrikes in Indian territory. In an air battle, an Indian pilot was captured by Pakistan. India and Pakistan were on the brink of a war over the release of the Pilot. After several days of tension, Pakistan returned the captured Pilot, Varthaman Abhinandan to India. No major developments occurred after the post Pulwama tensions.

Thus, we can see that there was a remarkable difference in the way PM Modi handled terror and Pakistan. For decades, India followed a weak policy towards Pakistan's covert war on India using terrorists. This approach changed after Modi took over. India has taken a zero-tolerance policy on cross-border terrorism from Pakistan. After the abolition of Article 370 and J&K being made Union Territory, directly ruled by the Central Government, internal security in Kashmir has been tightened and terrorists eliminated in targetted strikes. Border Security is maintained at maximum alert level and our defence forces keep a sharp eye on preventing terrorist infiltration from Pakistan.

China

India-China relations saw its ups and downs during the Modi era. Credit should be given to Modi for his earnest efforts to build relations with Xi-Jinping and China. During September 2017-19, Xi-Jinping had a 3 day state visit to India in Ahmedabad at the invitation of Modi. A budding bonhomie was on display between the two world leaders as Modi and Xi took a stroll along the Sabarmati Riverfront and sat side by side on a swing. Twelve agreements were signed between India and China. In May 2015, Modi became the first world leader to be hosted by Xi at his home town in Xian. The two sides held wide range of discussions on matters like terrorism and boundary dispute and confidence building measures at Summit level talks. In July 2015, in Russia, Modi held comprehensive discussions with Xi on bilateral ties. Modi raised strong concerns on China's decision to block UN action over Pakistan for releasing 26/11 attack mastermind Zakir-ur-Rehman Lakhvi.

In June, in Tashkent, Modi held his fourth meeting with Xi on the side-lines of SCO Summit. India had applied for membership of Nuclear Supplier Group that controls access to sensitive nuclear technology. Modi had urged China to have a fair and objective assessment of Indian application. China has since repeatedly opposed India's bid for entry into NSG.

On September 4, 2016, at the bilateral meeting with Xi, at the G20 Summit at Hangzhou, PM Modi raised India's concerns over the China-Pakistan Economic Corridor (CPEC) being laid through POK.

China vetoed India's petitions to blacklist Jaish-e-Mohammad Chief Masood Azhar in the UNSC.

Again, in October 2016, at the BRICS Summit in Goa, Modi and Xi met and had discussions on key issues including terrorism, NSG and enhancing trade and investment. The tone of the talks was positive.

On June 9, 2017, Modi and Xi again met at Astana, Kazakhstan at the SCO Summit.

Prior to the Summit, India had declined an invitation to Belt and Road Initiative hosted by Beijing.

It was reported that at the meeting at Astana, Chinese President had called for more high level interactions, Institutional exchange and Policy alignment between the two countries. (In this Summit, both India and Pakistan formally joined the SCO Security bloc spearheaded by China and Russia).

On July 7, 2017, Modi and Xi had an informal meeting at Hamburg, Germany. They had a conversation on a range of issues. This was the time when Indian and Chinese troops had a tense stand off at Doklam.

Doklam Stand off

After 73 days of stand off, Doklam issue was resolved through diplomatic channels. On September, 5, 2017, in Xiamen, China at the BRICS Summit, PM Modi and Xi Jinping held a substantial bilateral meeting. The two leaders re-affirmed their understanding that differences shouldn't be allowed to become disputes. At the Summit, China, for the first time, did not object to the listing of Pakistan based JEM, LeT and Haqqani Network as International Terror Groups.

During April 26-28, 2018, at Wuhan, China, Modi and Xi met informally where the two leaders had one on one interaction. Modi and Xi decided that they would issue guidance to their militaries to strengthen communications to build trust and understanding.(The Times of India June 08 2018)

Clash at Galwan Valley

On the night of Jun 15-16, 2020, the Indian Army and the People's Liberation Army clashed in a hand to hand combat at Galwan valley in Ladakh resulting in death of 20 Indian soldiers and unspecified number of casualties on the Chinese side. It was after 45 years that a clash along the LAC resulted in casualties. Indian and Chinese troops were engaged in a clash on the night of May5-6, 2020, at Pangong Tso in Ladakh. Another skirmish followed four days later at Naku La in Sikkim in the Eastern sector. These clashes occurred due to China's attempts to unilaterally alter the status quo on the LAC. China has been amassing large number of troops in Ladakh since early 2020, backed by tanks and armoured personnel carriers. These soldiers crossed into Indian territory at several points. In early June, Military Commanders of both sides agreed to pull back to create a buffer zone at Galwan Valley. On June 14, when Indian soldiers went to check if the PLA had withdrawn, they were attacked by Chinese soldiers. These incidents resulted in mutual suspicion. As a result of diplomatic, political and military talks, troops have disengaged from Galwan Valley, North and South banks of Pangong Tso Lake and the Gogra Hot springs area. However, disengagement from strategic Depsang Plains and Demchok has not happened yet. It is said that China is unwilling to discuss these two areas calling it 'legal issues'.

Both the countries differ on the way the situation is perceived. China is claiming that the situation is normalising in the borders whereas India is saying the situation is very fragile and quite dangerous.

On December 9, 2022, the two sides clashed near Tawang in the Eastern sector following a planned attempt by China to take control of a 17, 000 ft peak in the area. (The Times of India dated June 08, 2018) (thediplomat.com) and from various sources)

China, India's biggest trading partner

While border tensions, China's support to Pakistan at the UN on Pakistan sponsored terrorism in India and on NSG continue to bedevil Indo-China relations, China continues to be India's top trading partner. India's imports from China was a whopping US$118.77 billion whereas India's exports to China was only 17.49 billion with a trade deficit of US$ 101.28 billion in 2022. (eoi.beijing.gov.in).

QUAD

India is a member of the QUAD (Quadrilateral Security Dialogue), a strategic Forum comprising USA, Japan, Australia and India. The objective of QUAD is to keep the strategic sea routes in the Indo-Pacific free of any military influence. It aims to secure a rule based global border, freedom of navigation and a liberal trading system.

This forum is a bulwark to counter the aggressive military and economic expansion of China especially in the South China sea area and the Indo Pacific. (www.mea.gov.in)

Prime Minister Modi was active in the QUAD Summit hosted by President Biden in September 2021.

CHAPTER XII

G-20 Summit

India assumed the Presidency of G-20 on 1st December, 2022 for a period of one year.

Prime Minister Modi's exceptional leadership qualities and organisational skills were on display at the G-20 Presidency of India. In his inimitable style, every step that Modi takes is one more building block for India's progress. Around 200 G-20 meetings and events in over 30 different work streams comprising Sherpa Trade Working Groups, Finance Trade, Ministerial Meetings, Engagement Groups, were conducted in the length and breadth of the country showcasing India's vibrant history, culture, architecture, dance, music and India's economic progress. Over 1, 00, 000 participants from G-20 members, 9 invitee countries and 14 international organisations visited different parts of the country during these meetings.

Modi made G-20 Summit like celebration of a festival. Cities, towns and streets were beautified, flowering plants bedecked the routes to the meeting places, Indian arts, architecture ad cultural heritage were displayed at airports, venues, roads and new fountains installed. Citizens felt a sense of participation in the events. A new Exhibition-cum-Convention Centre called the Bharat Mandapam was built at Pragati Maidan, New Delhi at a cost of Rs.2000 crore where the G-20 Summit was held. It has a world class Convention Centre that can accommodate 7, 000 people in a single format.

The theme of India's G-20 Presidency was "Vasudhaiva Kutumbukam". One Earth, One Family, One Future underlying a message of equitable growth and a shared future for all.

The G-20 Summit under India's Presidency was a resounding success. In spite of nagging doubts whether a consensus declaration would be possible in the backdrop of conflicting views arising after the Ukraine-Russia war, it goes to the credit of India that a 100% consensus was adopted.

Again it goes to the credit of India that through out the Indian Presidency, the voice of Global South was given a prominent place in the meetings and in the Summit Declaration.

African Union

Under India's initiative, African Union has now become a Permanent Member of G-20.

India achieved a major feat by starting a Global Biofuel Alliance pact for Green development focussing on financing , cutting global green house gas emissions and ending plastic pollution. All the countries came together for this pact.

G-20 Declaration

The Summit declaration calls for

i. Accelerating strong, sustainable, balanced and inclusive growth
ii. Accelerate the full and effective implementation of the 2030 Agenda for Sustainable Development Goals.
iii. Pursue low/GHG/low carbon Emissions, to address climate challenges, promote Lifestyle for Sustainable Development (LIFE) and conserve biodiversity, forests and oceans.
iv. To improve access to medical supplies and production capacities in developing countries to prepare better for health emergencies.
v. To promote resilient growth by urgently addressing debt vulnerabilities in developing countries.
vi. Scale up financing for progress on SDGs
vii. Accelerate efforts towards achieving goals in Paris Agreement including temperature goal.
viii. Reforms for better, bigger and more effective Multilateral Development banks to address global challenges.
ix. To improve access to digital services and digital public infrastructure to boost sustainable growth.
x. To promote sustainable, quality, healthy, safe and gainful employment.
xi. Close gender gaps and promote full participation of women in the economy as decision makers.

xii. To better integrate the perspectives of developing countries into future G-20 Agenda and strengthen voice of developing countries in global decision making.

(www.g20.in) (www.mea.in)

CHAPTER XIII

India's Digital Revolution

"India achieved in 9 years what would have taken 47 years by traditional means"

Nandan Nilekani

Chairman and Co-founder, Infosys

And Founder Chairman, Aadhaar (UIDAI)

(Business Today, August 23, 2023)

Prime Minister Modi brought about a Digital Revolution in India in the last 9 ½ years. At the height of Covid 19 pandemic in 2021, when fear gripped all of us about transmission of infection through social contact, we used to order our essentials online, pay online and get delivered these items at our door step. Our milkman and vegetable vendor, both have digital payment facilities like Paytm, Phone Pe, GPay or a similar payment app. This adaptation of technology to the grassroots level, to the rediwalas, vegetable and fruit vendors, to the common man, was brought through the vision of PM Modi.

Modi had a fascination for new technologies and somehow realised the great potential of technology to transform the lives of people. When Modi was Chief Minister of Gujarat, in 2003, he had started the

SWAGAT (State-wide Attention on Grievances by Application of Technology) platform, an online grievances redressal system, one of the first in the country. In 2007, Chief Minister Modi had abolished paper files in the Gandhinagar Secretariat. We, Indians, who are used to hear excuses in Government Offices that this file or that file is untraceable and making endless rounds to such Offices and were forced to grease the palms of the Government Machinery, would understand the significance of such a far reaching step by Modi.

Digital India

After becoming PM, Modi used the technical insights that he gained as CM in Gujarat to replicate Pan India.

PM Modi launched the flagship programme of Digital India on July 1, 2015. The Programme is a vision to transform India into a digitally empowered Society and a Knowledge Economy.

The Programme envisages providing a Digital Infrastructure as a core utility to every citizen. Under this, availability of high speed internet, cradle to grave (birth to death) digital identity, mobile phone and bank accounts enabling citizens in digital and financial space and easy access to Common Service Centres, Governance and Services on Demand and Digital Empowerment of Citizens.

Aadhaar

Aadhaar or the Unique Identification Authorty of India ID, is a 12 digit unique identity number, based on biometrics and demographic data issued by the Government.

Aadhaar, started in 2009, was given a new role by PM Modi. In his unique style, PM Modi, leveraged the Aadhaar by using it to link the Mobile Phone number and bank account. Modi Govt had earlier launched the Jan Dhan Yojana by opening bank accounts for the crores of unbanked citizens of India.

By creating a JAM trinity (Jan Dhan A/c, Aadhaar Id and Mobile Phone), an unparalleled revolution was brought about in India for the common man. It may be recalled that the use of mobile phones by the people were rising rapidly. With the entry of private telecom players like Reliance Jio into the telecom market, India also witnessed a telecom revolution. Reliance Jio, that entered the market in 2016, disrupted the telecom market with it's aggressive pricing and data offerings. Data became cheaper. The JAM trinity was used to deliver Government's various Welfare Schemes by Direct Benefit Transfer (DBT) cutting out all intermediaries and corruption. Modi had stated "JAM is about achieving maximum value for every rupee spent, maximum empowerment for our poor, maximum technological penetration among the masses".

There were over 1.2 billion mobile phone users and over 600 million smartphone users in India as of November 2022, according to Secretary, Ministry of Information and Broadcasting. (pib.gov.in press release dated 16 Nov 2022)

There are over 135.5 crore residents having Aadhaar IDs. 326 schemes are currently in use, transferring benefits directly into the bank accounts of the beneficiaries. A total of Rs. 20.23 lakh crore had been transferred into the bank accounts of beneficiaries till end December 2021. It is estimated that Government saved over 2 lakh crore by eliminating bogus and fake accounts and ghost beneficiaries.

UPI

Ever since Modi Government took over, concerted effort was on by all Govt. agencies to push the financial transactions from cash based to formal banking channels. We remember black money was a bane and a hurdle to India's economic progress.

Demonetisation and Digitisation of Financial Transactions

Modi took the bold step of demonetisation in 2016 and simultaneously encouraged citizens to use cashless transactions.

UPI or Unified Payments Interface (BHIM Bharat Interface for Money) is the digital payment platform that Government developed through the National Payments Corporation of India.

With India's banking sector comprising the Public and Private sector Banks joining hands with fintech companies from the Private sector like Paytm, Phone Pe, Bharat Pe, a new financial eco-system came up where citizens could use a phone based app to make payments and receive payments. So, in the length and breadth of the country, you go to a shop or a small-time vendor of vegetables/fruits/food items, a QR code is displayed in front through which a payment is made in a fraction of a second. No need to take out your wallet, take out cash and pay and take back change. Time is saved, there is digital record of payment, no need to worry about transmission of Covid or any other infections through the currency notes.

More than 376 banks are operational on UPI now. Transactions worth 11.9 lakh crore have been made using UPI.

The digital transactions leave a digital footprint and the Govt. is using its digital footprint to promote credit facility to the users (pib.gov.in on 23 Dec 2022).

As per an IMF sponsored study, www.IMF.org says with nearly a billion internet users in India, a host of indigenous digital services, platforms, applications, content and solutions, are expected to transform the digital ecosystem in India. India could potentially see a five fold increase in economic value by digital transformation by 2025.

Common Service Centres

Common Service Centres are offering Government and Business services in digital mode in rural areas through Village Level Entrepreneurs (VLE). Over 400 digital services are being offered by these CSCs. 5.21 lakh CSCs are functioning including urban and rural, out of which 4.14 lakh CSCs are functioning at Gram Panchayat Level.

Digi Lockers

Digital lockers provide an ecosystem to upload documents in the digital depositories. This can be done both by the issuers of such documents as well as by individuals holding documents like Aadhaar, Driving License, Passports, Property documents, etc.

As of now 13.7 crore users and more than 562 crore documents are made available through Digi Lockers from 2, 311 issuer organisations.

Certified Mobile Application for New Age Governance (UMANG)

This is for providing government services to citizens through mobile. Here 1668 e-services and over 20, 197 bill payment services are available on UMANG.

E-Sign

E-sign service facilitates instant signing of forms / documents online by citizens in a legally acceptable form.

MyGov – is a citizen engagement portal to facilitate participatory governance. Over 2.76+ crore users are registered with MyGov, participating in various activities hosted on MyGov platform.

Meri Pehchan

National single sign-on (NSSO) platform called Meri Pehchan was launched in July, 2022 to facilitate/promote citizens ease of access to government portals. 4, 419 services of various Ministries / States are integrated with NSSO.

Digital Village

700 Gram Panchayats are covered under this project. At least one Gram Panchayat/village per district comes under the project. The Digital services offered are Digital Health Services, Skill Development, etc.

E-District

Mission Mode Project for electronic delivery of citizen centre service at District/Sub district level. 709 Districts are offering these services.

CHAPTER XIV

Making Possible the Impossible

Article 370

The State of J&K joined the Indian Union on October 26, 1947, after signing the Instrument of Accession by Maharaja Hari Singh.

On October, 17, 1949, a special provision of Article 370 was incorporated in the Constitution to provide Special Status to the state of J&K giving the state autonomy. The Article clearly stated that the provision was a temporary feature and the President of India had the powers to revoke it.

For 72 years, the temporary provision continued and the real integration of the State with the Indian Union did not happen. During these 72 years, Kashmir was a festering wound on the body politic of the country. Terrorism supported by Pakistan, call for independence by some bodies, burning of Indian flag, stoning Indian Army and Central Police Forces and a host of other anti-Indian activities thrived in J&K. Most of the time normal life was affected because of such an atmosphere affecting the education of children, economic development of the state and real integration of the state with the Union of India.

It took a great and visionary leader like Narendra Modi, ably supported by his Home Minister, Amit Shah to take the bold step of revoking Article 370 ending the special status of J&K. On August 5, 2019, Modi Government struck down Article 370 and bifurcated the state into two Union Territories of Jammu and Kashmir and Ladakh.

On December 11, 2023, the Supreme Court upheld the Government's decision.

The abrogation of Article 370 was a historic step by the Narendra Modi Government.

Ram Mandir in Ayodhya

According to the Epic, Ramayana, Lord Shree Ram, one of the Avatars of Lord Vishnu, was born in Ayodhya, on the banks of River Sarayu.

A temple of Lord Shree Ram that existed at the birth place of Shree Ram at Ayodhya was demolished on the orders of Mughal emperor Babur and built a mosque there known as Babri masjid.

(It is mentioned in Babur Nama, translated from the original Turki text by Annette Susannah Beveridge- Appendices U-XXVII -Foot Note -3-The Inscriptions inside Babur's Mosque in Ajodhya (Oudh)-"Mir Baqi of Tashkint.Perhaps a better epithet for sa'adat-nishan than good hearted" would be one implying his good fortune in being designated to build a mosque on the site of the ancient Hindu Temple". Further at Foot Note I- U-

XXVIII, it is mentioned, "presumably the order for building the mosque was given during Babur's stay in Aud(Ajodhya) in 934 AH(1528 AD) at which time he would be impressed by the dignity and sanctity of the ancient Hindu shrine it, at least in part displaced, and like the obedient follower he was in intolerance of another Faith, would regard the substitution of a temple by a mosque as dutiful and worthy". It may be mentioned here that these are interpretations of the Translator and not literal translation of the inscriptions.

In 1980, the Vishwa Hindu Parishad (VHP) and other Hindu nationalist groups and political parties launched a campaign to construct the Ram Janmabhoomi Mandir at the site.

If we calculate from the time Arabs overran the Kingdom of Raja Dabir of Sindh in 715 CE to Bahadur Shah Zafar II, the last and the 20 th Emperor of Mughal rule in India in 1857, India, i.e., Bharat, faced Islamic invasions and their rule for over 1, 000 years. Of Course there are interludes in between. As the Islamic rulers were true to their faith, Hindus were subjected to coercion and force. These scars on Hindu psyche continued even after India's independence because of a false or pseudo sense of secularism. It is noteworthy that no ruler of India since independence tried to sympathise or empathise with the Hindus with the exception of Atal Bihari Vajpayee.

Then came Narendra Modi as the PM of India in 2014. Unlike most of the other politicians in India who don a Hindu Tilak or a Janeyu in the morning visiting a temple, wearing a skull cap and visiting a masjid at noon and wearing a cross and visiting a church in the evening, Modi wore his Hinduism on his sleeve. No Secularism trap. Wherever he goes, he visits the prominent temples in that area. In the last 9 1/2 years, he was instrumental in developing the Char-dham project, the Kashi Vishwanath Corridor, Mahakaal Corridor and restore the great glory of these Hindu places of worship.

It is very important to mention here that as PM, Shri Narendra Modi meticulously follows the Constitution of India and treats all faiths with reverence and Government of India's developmental Schemes follow the principle of "Sab Ka Saath, Sab Ka Vikas, Sab Ka Vishwas and Sab ka Prayas".

Back to Ram Temple in Ayodhya. Narendra Modi as an RSS Kartyakarta travelled to hundreds of villages in Gujarat to gather signatures in support of building a Ram Temple in Ayodhya between February 1993 and June 1993. He gathered 10 crore signatures and played a key role in the signature campaign organised at that time.

After becoming the Organisational Secretary of the BJP in Gujarat in 1987, Modi teamed up with VHP Chief Parvin Togadia to popularise the Ram Temple movement in the state. In 1989, Modi helped the VHP to organise the Ram Shila Puja.

Narendra Modi also played a key role as a frontline organiser of Shri L.K. Advani's Rath yatra from Somnath to Ayodhya in September 1990. He also organised the Gujarat leg of the yatra through 600 villages of Gujarat and followed it as far as Mumbai.

Modi wanted a Constitutional resolution to the Ram Temple issue. The Supreme Court's unanimous decision in favour of handing over the disputed 2.77 acre plot and the 67.703 acre land acquired under the Ayodhya Act 1993 to the Ram Janmabhoomi Nyas for construction of a Ram Temple, was a victory for all those who were involved in the Ram Janmabhoomi Movement including Modi. SC also directed the Central Government under PM Modi to constitute a Ram Janmbhoomi Teerth Kshetra Trust for the construction and management of the Ram Temple. PM Modi announced the formation of the Trust in the Lok Sabha on 5 February 2020. It is noteworthy that former Principal Secretary to the Prime Minister, Shri Nripendra Misra is in charge of the Ram Temple Construction in Ayodhya as the present Chairman of the Trust.

The Shilanyas of the temple was performed on 5 August 2020 by PM Modi and the construction of the temple started thereon. The temple is designed as per the Hindu texts, the Vastu Shastra and the Shilpa Shastras. The temple and the surrounding areas of Ayodhya will reflect the ancient civilisational and sacred glory of Lord Ram's abode when completed.

The Prana Pratishta (consecration) ceremony of the Ram Temple took place on 22 January 2024 led by PM Modi. This day was celebrated in India and all over the world with great enthusiasm like Diwali to herald the home coming of Lord Shree Ram.

Implementation of GST

The idea of introducing a One Nation One Tax and one Market, was mooted in the year 2000. The objective was to integrate State Taxes with different rates on the same commodities and services and the Central Excise duty, various cesses and additional surcharges, State Value Added Tax, Central Sales Tax, Purchase Tax, Entry Tax etc into one Goods and Services Tax. A Constitution Amendment Bill was introduced in Parliament in 2014. After very long and complex negotiations with the State Governments, the requisite Constitution Amendment Act was passed and enacted in 2016. GST Council was notified in 2016 and the GST laws were implemented in July 2017. There was stiff resistance to the implementation of GST by the Opposition parties.

It took 17 years and a concerted push by the Modi government for the implementation of GST. GST is a unified, efficient and transparent indirect Tax regime that contributed immensely in the ease of doing business in India.Implementtion of GST is another step towards national integration.The long lines of trucks at the Entry Tax plazas is a thing of the past.

GST collections are averaging more than Rs 1,50,000 crore a month enhancing the revenue collections of both the Centre and the States and helping in the development of the country.

CHAPTER XV

Great Leaders are Great Builders too

During Narendra Modi's Chief Ministership in Gujarat and later as the PM of India, he built some iconic buildings and structures.

The Statue of Unity in Kevadia, Gujarat

The Statue of Unity, an iconic 182 metres tall Iron Statue, the World's tallest statue, was built as a tribute to Sardar Vallabhai Patel, the first Home Minister of India in Kevadia (renamed Ekta Nagar), Gujarat. As we know, Sardar Patel, also known as the Iron Man of India, was instrumental in uniting 565 princely states of India to the Indian Union with his steadfast commitment to National Integration.

Narendra Modi proposed the ambitious project of building the Statue of Unity to his Cabinet in 2010 and laid the foundation stone on 31 October 2013, when he was the Chief Minister of Gujarat. On October 31, 2018, exactly 5 years later Modi inaugurated the Statue of Unity.

A Statue of Unity Movement was started in 2013 to collect iron for the Statue. Sardar Patel was closely associated with the farming community and had led many movements for the farmers. For the Iron statue in memory of the Iron man of India, iron was collected from farmers across country. Used farm tools and soil samples were collected from 1, 69, 078 locations across the country as a symbolic gesture of National unity and thus collected 135 tonnes of iron for the project.

A visit to the Statue of Unity in Ekta Nagar brings to focus the genius, vision, patriotism and national fervour of PM Modi. The entire project is on the theme of national unity.

Narendra Mcdi Stadium

The idea of building a World class Cricket stadium in Motera in Ahmedabad on the banks of Sabarmati river reconstructing the existing one was proposed by Narendra Modi when he was the President of the Gujarat Cricket Association and the Chief minister of Gujarat. This was Narendra Modi's dream project also. The result was the building of the World's largest stadium with a seating capacity of 1, 32, 000 spectators. Built at a cost closer to 800 crores, the stadium is owned by the Gujarat Cricket Association. The Association named the stadium as the Narendra Modi Stadium.

The Narendra Modi stadium is one more example of the vision of PM Modi for making India great.

The Central Vista Project

The Modi Government also embarked on an ambitious project to revamp and refurbish the Central Vista which is the heart of Delhi and that of India by building new infrastructure for India's Parliament, a Central Secretariat to house all 51 Ministries of the Government of India, new Prime Minister's office, Residence and Vice President's Residence.(https://centralvista.gov.in)

New Parliament Building.

As part of the Central vista Project, a state of the art New Parliament Building with a built up area of 65, 000 sq, mt in triangular shape has been built and was inaugurated on 28 May 2023 by Prime Minister Narendra Modi. The new Parliament House has larger chambers for legislatures. A larger Lok Sabha Hall with a capacity of 888 seats, three times bigger compared to the old parliament House with better ease of sitting for Members. It has a larger Rajya Sabha Hall with a capacity of 384 seats. It has a state of the Art Constitution hall, ultra modern office spaces, large Committee Rooms equipped with latest audio-visual systems and a new Parliament Building Library. There is also a Central Lounge for members to interact. The new Parliament House reflects the vibrancy and diversity of modern India and incorporates the Cultural heritage of India with regional arts and crafts. At the inauguration of the new Parliament House, following a Tamil tradition, a gold plated sceptre, Sengol, a symbol of just rule, was installed near the Chair of the Speaker of Lok Sabha. (https://centalvista.gov.in)

Kartavya Path

The stretch of 3 kms from Rashtrapati Bhawan to India Gate, earlier known as Rajpath, has been renamed as Kartavya Path and has been refurbished and infrastructure upgraded with new social amenities retaining its essential character. The lawn space on either side of Kartavya Path has been increased from 3, 50, 000 sq ft to 3, 90, 000 sq ft. All the existing trees continue to enhance the beauty of Kartavya Path. All the water bodies have been refurbished. The revamped Kartavya Path is attracting large number of visitors. According to the Union Minister for Housing and Urban Affairs, Hon'ble Hardeep Singh Puri, an average of 1, 25, 000 to 1, 50, 000 visitors on weekends and 70, 000 on weekdays visit Kartavya Path belying the critics who claimed that the revamp of Kartavya Path would deprive the citizens of their favourite weekend destination for relaxation. (https://centralvista, gov.in)

Bharat Mandapam

The Bharat Mandapam is a world -class facility equipped with modern infrastructure and technology suitable for summits, meetings, cultural events etc. The Convention Centre has dedicated VIP and guest lounges and five star catering services to host up to 7, 000 persons.

Bharat Mandapam was built as a part of the comprehensive revamp plan of Pragati Maidan. The International Exhibition and Convention Centre was conceptualised and built by ITPO(India Trade Promotion Organisation) as per the direction of Prime Minister Narendra Modi in December 2015 at a cost of Rs 2600 crore.

The different walls and facades of the Convention Centre depict various facets of India's traditional art and culture.The Centre is adorned with paintings and tribal art forms from different parts of the country. A 27 ft tall bronze statue of Nataraja was also installed at Bharat Mandapam.

The G-20 Summit, hosted by India for the first time, was held at Bharat Mandapam. India's rich history, culture and heritage were depicted at the venue with art installations, fountains and lights leaving a lasting impression on the thousands of participants in the G-20 summit.

The timely completion of the iconic Bharat Mandapam and holding of a very successful G-20 Summit at this venue is testimony to the forethought and vision of PM Modi.(https://indiatradefair.com)

Yashobhoomi (India International Convention and Expo Centre)

Another iconic project that the Modi Government is executing is India's largest Convention and Expo Centre at Dwarka Sector 25, in New Delhi. When completed, it will have a total of 3, 00, 000 sq.mt of Convention and Exhibition space and 1 million sq.mt of total multi-purpose Development including hotels, offices, shopping centres and entertainment facilities.

Upon completion of Phase II of the Project, the Centre will have five large exhibition halls, a multi-purpose convention Centre with the largest auditorium in India capable of holding 6, 000 people at a time as well as multi-purpose arena facilities for 20, 000 people. 3, 500 guest rooms will be available within 1 km.

Phase I of the Project is already complete. A state of the Art Metro Station connecting the Airport Metro Line has already been opened for use. The Dwarka Expressway and Urban Extension Road II will give seamless connectivity from Yashobhoomi to Delhi Airport, Central and other parts of Delhi and Gurgaon. Delhi Blue line Metro is adjacent to the Centre.

Being built at a cost of Rs 25,700 crore, Yashobhoomi is one of those projects taking India to the league of a developed country.

The futuristic vision of PM Modi is clear in this project.

(https://www.iiccnewdelhi.com)

Refurbishing Temples

In addition to the grand Ram Temple being built and consecrated in Ayodhya, many other temples and their surroundings have been refurbished, new corridors built and access roads have been constructed in the last 9 ½ years.

Kashi Vishwanath Corridor

To revamp and beautify the entire surroundings of Kashi Vishwanath temple, a Kashi Vishwanath temple Extension and beautification plan was launched in 2019.The ambitious project included connecting the temple to the ghats of river Ganga with a paved walkway, 320 metres long and 20 metres wide, removal of encroachments in the immediate vicinity of the temple, construction of facilities like Yatri Suvidha Kendra(Tourist Facilitation Centre), Mumuksha bhawan (Salvation home), Mandir Chowk, a museum, a library, auditorium, bhogsala, shops, cafes and public conveniences. Around three hundred buildings spread over 50,000 square metres were acquired and demolished by the authorities. While removing the encroachments, several forgotten temples and religious sanctuaries were found. Around thirty temples have been restored to their former splendour.

Kashi, believed to be the oldest city of India has been given a massive facelift and restored to its old glory. PM Modi inaugurated the Corridor Project in December 2021.

Mahakaleshwar Temple Corridor Project

Mahakaleshwar Temple in Ujjain is one of the 12 Jyotirlingas of Shiva. The redevelopment project around the ancient temple includes development of a 900 metre long "Mahakal Lok" corridor, revival of the Rudrasagar lake, decongestion and beautification of temple precincts and expansion of the surrounding areas substantially. The cost of the entire project is Rs 850 crore. Two majestic gateways-Nandi Dwar and Pinaki Dwar have been erected near the starting point of the corridor which leads to the entrance of the temple. A majestic colonnade of 108 ornate pillars made of intricately carved sandstones and a running panel of over 50 murals depicting stories from Shiv Purana enhance the beauty of the Corridor. The Corridor gives a divine experience to the lakhs of devotees thronging the temple. The first phase of the project was inaugurated by PM Modi on 11 October 2022.

Char Dham Mahamarg Vikas Pariyojana

A flagship project of the Ministry of Road Transport and Highways, the Project includes widening and improvement of 825 km of National Highways for faster and safer road connectivity from Rishikesh to Yamunotri, Gangotri, Gaurikund (Kedarnath) and Mana (Badrinath) including Tanakpur to Pithoragarh section of Kailash Mansarovar route in Uttarakhand. The estimated cost of the Project is Rs 12, 072 crores.

The foundation stone of the Project was laid by PM Modi in December 2016. According to a written reply to the Rajya Sabha on 26 July 2023, Union Minister for Road transport and Highways, Shri Nitin Gadkari, informed that out of 825 km, about 601 km had been completed. The Minister also informed that the NH projects in Uttarakhand faced delays due to delay in land acquisition, forest clearance, tree cutting, litigation etc. (pib.gov.in Press Release dated 26 July2023). It may be mentioned that adverse weather conditions also is a big challenge to the Project.

CHAPTER XVI

Connecting with People

Mann Ki Baat

Mann Ki Baat is a unique Radio Programme started by Prime Minister Modi in 2014 to connect with the people of India. Such a programme is unprecedented in the history of India. No other Prime Minister of India ever tried such a way to be in touch with the vast population of India on themes and issues of non-political nature.

Mann Ki Baat is a kaleidoscope of the different and vibrant colours of India. The programme covers such subjects that we ordinarily do not come to know through the mainstream media. It brings to the notice of citizens unique ideas and successes of people in multifarious fields.

Just a few examples of some of the subjects covered in a single programme of 30 minutes. Water conservation efforts across India started by people from different walks of life in different parts of the country. Cleaning and rejuvenating waterbodies, ponds, streams and rivers. Digging new ponds to conserve water. Rainwater harvesting in different parts of the country. Building of small dams by Panchayats. Reviving stepwells. References to various festivals celebrated in different parts of the country. References to great successes by women in different fields from different parts of the country. Reference to making cloth from hitherto unheard of sources like bamboo, plantain trees etc. Unique library movements started by youngsters. Caring of animals by community efforts. Memorials to national leaders, paintings of national leaders by individuals. Conserving the history and culture of India. Conserving the traditions of India. Achievements in various sports by youngsters in national and International events. New methods adopted in agriculture. Efforts to clean beaches, rivers, roads, stadiums, roads, etc by community efforts. Teaching children and illiterates by exceptional individuals. Promotion of Yoga and fitness among people. Promotion and participation in International Day of Yoga. Contribution to Music and literature by many stalwarts. Miyawaki method of afforestation for sustainable growth. Ni-kshay Mitras making the fight against TB. Extra-ordinary efforts by Doctors, nurses and paramedics and community participation in the fight against Covid 19 pandemic. Fights against natural disasters by NDRF and many voluntary bodies.

Mann Ki Baath is like a conversation with the family of Indians. It is inspirational, educative, informative and always very interesting. Every word and sentence to better people's lives and taking the nation to greater heights.

Pariksha Pe Charcha

Prime Minister Modi has been interacting with students, teachers and parents across the country since 2018 on how to give Examinations without getting stressed. During this annual event, generally before the board and various entrance examinations, Prime Minister gives valuable tips to students as to how to stay calm during the Examination time and how physical activities like yoga, meditation and games help in building the mental ability to be tension free. These interactions exhort parents and teachers not to put pressure on children while preparing for examinations. The Prime Minister has also penned a book "Exam Warriors" on this subject. Written in a fun and interactive style, with illustrations, this book is a good friend to youngsters in facing examinations.

Social Media

Twitter (Now X)

PM Modi has been very active on the Social Media. As of 26 January 2024, PM Modi has 94.8 million (9.48 crore) followers.

Instagram

PM Modi has 86.1 Million (8.61 crores) followers on Instagram.

Narendra Modi App

PM Modi launched an official Narendra Modi App on 17 June 2015, an interactive App where updates on PM Modi's day-to-day activities are available. Citizens are also encouraged to give suggestions and opinions on various initiatives of the Government on this App.

PM Modi has been able to connect with the people through his unique initiatives like Mann Ki Baat, Parikhsha Pe Charcha and through Namo App. It is also said that a large number of people connect to him through letters and e mail.

CHAPTER XVII

Women Empowerment

Prime Minister Modi has been giving a lot of attention to gender equality, women empowerment and women led development.

As Chief Minister of Gujarat, Modi had made sterling efforts to promote Girl child education through schemes like "Kanya Kelavani Nidhi" (Girl Child Education) and "Shala Praveshotsav" (School Enrolment Festival). In 2011, then CM Modi, in an unprecedented move, mobilised his Ministers, Secretaries, Government officials and people's representatives and visited schools in 18, 000 villages, 151 municipalities and 8 Municipal Corporations for assessment of Government primary school enrolments and quality of education especially for girl children.

(https//www.narendramodi.in), (deshgujarat.com)

Modi Government at the Centre launched the "Beti Bachao Beti Padhao" Scheme in January 2015 to address concerns about discrimination against girl child and for women empowerment. "Save the girl child, educate the girl child" was a nationwide campaign to ensure survival and protection of the girl child and encourage education of girl child. Multi Sectoral interventions were implemented in gender critical districts across the country. The 'selfie with daughter' campaign was successful in educating the society on how the girl child was treated by them.(myScheme.gov.in)

Sukanya Samridhi Yojana launched by the Government as a part of the Beti bachao Beti padhao Scheme is a money deposit scheme meant exclusively for a girl child meant to meet her education and marriage expenses. In the Scheme, a minimum of Rs 1, 000 and a maximum of Rs 1, 50, 000 can be deposited for a girl child who attained the age of 10. The Scheme offers a higher interest on the deposit and Income Tax savings. Benefit of annual compounding is also given by the scheme. As per a PIB release dated january20, 2022, a total of 1, 42, 73, 910 accounts have been opened under the Scheme till 31.10.21. (static.pib.gov.in)

Swachh Bharat Mission has resulted in 14, 67, 679 schools having a functional girl's toilet that encouraged enrolment of girl students who were either not joining schools or were dropping out from schools.

Two major schemes of the Modi Government, Swachh Bharat Mission and the PM Ujjwala Yojana, have helped in remarkable improvement in women's health and sanitation. Under the Jal Jeevan Mission, Government is planning to give quality tap water to every household across the country which will substantially improve the ease of living for women. The drudgery of walking long distances to fetch water for daily consumption will become a thing of the past for women, especially the rural women.

(https//9years.mygov.in)(https.static.pib.gov.in)

PM Modi also initiated steps to improve women's menstrual health by providing access to menstrual hygiene products at low cost. Under Pradhan Mantri Bharatiya Janaushadi Pariyojana, Government had launched Jan Aushadi Suvidha Sanitary Pads at Re 1 per piece for easy availability of menstrual health products to poor women at affordable prices. Since inception in August 2019 till 30 November 2023, over 47.87 crore such pads have been sold through 10, 000 Jan Aushadi Kendras. (www.pib.gov.in release dated 08 Dec2023.)

Out of the 51.55 crore PM Jan Dhan Account holders, most of the beneficiaries are women making them part of the Financial/Banking system. This was a major step towards financial inclusion and empowerment of women. During the Covid 19 lockdown, because of the Jan Dhan Yojana accounts, money was transferred under Direct Benefit Transfer to the beneficiaries.

Under the PM Awas Yojana, Modi Government decided to give ownership of houses under this Scheme to the women further empowering them.

Pradhan Mantri Matru Vandana Yojana launched in 2017 gives Direct Benefit Transfer for pregnant women and lactating mothers. Under the Scheme, Rs 5, 000 is provided to the eligible beneficiary in three instalments during pregnancy and lactation. (pib.gov.in dated 04 February 2022). More than 3.11 crore beneficiaries are enrolled under this Scheme and maternity benefits of Rs 12, 150 crore have been disbursed to over 2.77 crore beneficiaries as on 21-11-2022.(pib.gov.in dated 16 December 2022).

Poradhan Mantri Mudra Yojana launched in 2015 gives credit of up to Rs 10 lakhs to small entrepreneurs. This Scheme targets young educated or skilled workers or entrepreneurs including women entrepreneurs. As per a report, 30.64 crore loans under this Scheme or 68% of the loans, was given to women as of 24 November 2023.This has helped crores of women across the country to pursue micro-level entrepreneurship and become financially independent. (with inputs from static.pib.gov.in)

Mission Poshan is an integrated nutrition support programme to address the challenges of malnutrition in children, adolescent girls, pregnant women and lactating mothers. As per this programme fortified rice is being supplied and millets are included in the meals supplied to beneficiaries through Anganwadis. The mission has been rolled out across all the 36 states and UTs. It covers 730 districts including 112 Aspirational districts.

Mission Shakti: Government has launched Mission Shakti, a scheme in Mission mode for strengthening interventions for women's safety, security and empowerment. It seeks to realise Government's commitment for 'women led development" by addressing issues affecting women and taking steps to make them equal partners in nation-building. Under Mission Shakti, many of the present Schemes focusing on women will be brought under this umbrella Scheme for women.(https://wcd.nic.in)

The impact of various schemes to improve health and quality of life of women is evident in the outcomes like improved sex ratio at birth which is for the first time 1020 women per 1000 men, a rise in institutional deliveries, declining Infant Mortality and a lower Maternal Mortality Rate. Maternal Mortality Rate fell from 167 per 1, 00, 000 live births in 2011-12 to 97 per 1, 00, 000 live births in 2018 -20 as per information shared with Rajya Sabha by MOS, Union Ministry of Health and Family Welfare. (downtoearth.org.in)

Ayushman Mahila Yojana was launched to encourage women, especially from rural areas to screen for diseases like cancer. With the Creation of Health and Wellness Centres across the country, 14.8 crore women have benefitted from the Ayushman Mahila Yojana.

Pradhan Mantri Surakshit Matritva Abhiyan is another Scheme focused on women, launched in 2016 to ensure safe and healthy ante-natal care to all pregnant women with private doctor services for free check up each month. 4.27 crore ante-natal check-ups have been conducted under this scheme. (pmsma.mohfw.gov.in)

Muslim Women(Protection of Rights on Marriage) Act 2019 made Triple Talaq illegal empowering the Muslim Women.(https://pib.gov.in)

Maternity Benefits Act was amended by Modi Government in 2019 to raise fully paid maternity leave from 12 weeks to 26 weeks in Organised Sector.

Under the 2013 Companies Act, it was made compulsory to have at least one female Director on the Boards of Companies.

Modi Government took several measures to give greater access to women in various fields to raise gender equality. Women have been granted Permanent Commission in all branches of Armed Forces. There are women Pilots in both Air Force and Navy. In May 2021, the Army inducted the first batch of women in the Corps of Military Police. On Independence Day 2021, PM Modi announced that girls would be given entry in Sainik Schools.

In the recent Chandrayaan -3 Mission of ISRO, from design to landing, over 100 women played a direct and significant role in making the soft-landing of Vikram on the lunar South Pole possible.(Times of India 25 August 23)

Women's Reservation in Lok Sabha and State legislatures.

In a landmark initiative by the Modi Government, the long pending Women's Reservation Bill was passed by Parliament on 21 September 2023 and enacted into law. Under this Act termed as the Nari Shakti Vandan Adhiniyam, 1/3 rd of the total seats in the Lok Sabha and the State Legislatures will be reserved for women. This is a major step towards women empowerment.

In showing Modi Government's resolve to empower women, the just concluded Republic Day Parade on 26 January 2024, was led by women contingents from all wings of the Armed Forces, Paramilitary, Police, NCC, NSS and the Cultural troupes. Even the daredevil teams of motorcyclists of the Armed Forces and paramilitary displaying acrobatics were entirely composed of women.

In the last 9 years and 8 months of Modi Government, with initiatives like Khelo India and Target Olympic Podium Scheme, concerted efforts were made to encourage sporting talent in the country and scores of women athletes were trained for National and International events. There has been a steady increase in the number of women sportspersons achieving medals in major International sporting events. In the Tokyo Olympics in 2021, PV Sindhu, Saikhom Mirabai Chanu and Lovlina Borgohain made India proud by winning medals. Our women sportspersons are doing exceptionally well in all sports and games.

CHAPTER XVIII

Youth and Sports

Prime Minister Modi had famously said "The image of a country is not just about economic and military strength. The soft face of a country also makes a difference. Sports is one such soft power which can capture the world's attention to India"

India has one of the youngest populations in the world. It is estimated that our youth population is about 65% of our population of 142 crore. There is a close linkage between Youth and Sports.

In the 2008 Beijing Olympics, India had 57 athletes, won 3 medals and ranked 50th in the World. In the 2012 London Olympics, 83 athletes participated, won 6 medals and was in the 55th position. In the 2016 Rio de Janeiro Olympics, India sent 117 athletes, won 2 medals and was in the 67th position. In the 2020 Tokyo Olympics, after almost a century, India performed better with 126 athletes, 7 medals and secured 48th position.

For a country with the largest population in the world, our achievements in the world of Sports and games is hardly anything to talk about. Excellence in sports and games is a barometer of the health of the nation, the level of its economic and social development, its nutritional standards, availability of infrastructure and overall growth orientation of the country.

The good news is that the Modi government has been taking measures to bring fundamental changes to nurture our talent and create world class infrastructure, training, nutritional support, financial assistance and career opportunities in sports.

The Mission Olympic Cell (MOC) was formed in April 2016 to provide impetus to Indian athletes competing in Olympics. To promote Sporting Excellence among elite athletes, Target Olympic Podium Scheme (TOPS) which was initially started in 2014, was revamped to address the further requirements of MOC. Under this Scheme, professional teams including research analysts, athlete relationship managers, sports science and sports-specific experts were brought on board to create a focussed support system for elite athletes. Measures taken included personalised coaching support from best global coaches, out of pocket Allowance of Rs 50, 000 per month per athlete in the Core Group and Rs 25, 000 per athlete in the Developmental Group, dedicated relationship manager as bridge between Sports Authority of India and athlete, foreign exposure, top-of-the-line research support to track opponent performance, sports science support, international training sessions and personalised equipment support.

Exclusive sports league for women at the grassroots level and support to elite women athletes has risen from 48 in 2015 to 178 in 2021. Financial support to host international competition for women is also being given.

Specialised sports infrastructure for athletes with disabilities is also being created.

Khelo India Scheme

Government started the Khelo India Scheme to create a national level platform for athletes to showcase their talent and to identify them for further grooming and financial support. From 2017 to 2020, 3 editions of Khelo India School and University games have been hosted giving talented sportspersons a chance to win a Khelo India Scholarship and be trained for higher levels of competition by best coaches in state-of -the art Sporting Complexes. 18, 000 athletes have participated in the Khelo India games and 2970 athletes have been chosen as Khelo India Athletes (KIAs) and are undergoing training in Khelo India Academies and revamped SAI Centres. These athletes are given Rs 10, 000 Out of Pocket Allowance besides being supported for training, equipment, diet and education. A funding of Rs 6.28 lakh per annum per athlete is made for these 2970 athletes.

235 Academies have been accredited for Khelo India Athletes in 21 disciplines.

Compared to 38 Sports Infrastructure Projects between 2010 and 2014, there are 267 Sports Infrastructure Projects developed during 2014 and 2020.

FIT India Movement

To realise Prime Minister's vision of a FIT India, a FIT India Movement was launched by the PM in August 2019. FIT India movement was first of its kind Movement in the History of India. Bringing together experts from the field of fitness and involving Corporates, Ministries of Education, Panchayati Raj, Health and Ayush, a people's movement was started to encourage people especially the youth to lead a lifestyle of fitness.

On 2nd October 2019, on the 150th Birth Anniversary of Mahatma Gandhi, a FIT India Plog (jogging while picking up plastic and other waste) run was organised which saw a participation of 30 lakh people.

A FIT India Cyclothon was organised between December 2020 to January 2021 that saw a participation of 1.2 crore people.

A FIT India Freedom Run was organised to celebrate the 74 th Independece Day and the 151st birth anniversary of Mahatma Gandhi in 2020 where people could run at a place and pace of their choice. Over 7 crore people participated in this run.

(http://yas.nic.in)

Prime Minister Modi closely interacts with our sportspersons and motivates them to do their best in international competitions. He invites them to his residence before major sports events and after. With the initiatives of the Modi Government and attractive cash awards being offered by the state Governments, there is a new enthusiasm among the youth to take sports and games as a career. With the recent World Cup Cricket played in India and India putting up a spectacular show in the game, India's traditional love for cricket continues. Both our men's and women's teams are doing exceptionally well in all our traditionally strong areas like cricket, wrestling, boxing, kabbadi etc. In shooting our boys and girls are breaking new records. In Chess, record number of Grand Masters are emerging.

India finished Asian Games 2023 with a record haul of 107 medals.28 gold, 38 silver and 41 bronze.

In sports and games also, a new enthusiasm and energy is emerging in India.

www.ingramcontent.com/pod-product-compliance
Lightning Source LLC
LaVergne TN
LVHW061617070526
838199LV00078B/7319